J
FICTION
SMITH

Smith, Jane Denitz.

Fairy dust.

DATE		

Fairy Dust

Jane Denitz Smith

Fairy Dust

 HarperCollinsPublishers

Fairy Dust
Copyright © 2002 by Jane Denitz Smith
All rights reserved. No part of this book may be used or repro-
duced in any manner whatsoever without written permission
except in the case of brief quotations embodied in critical arti-
cles and reviews. Printed in the United States of America. For
information address HarperCollins Children's Books, a division
of HarperCollins Publishers, 1350 Avenue of the Americas,
New York, NY 10019.
                    www.harperchildrens.com

Library of Congress Cataloging-in-Publication Data
Smith, Jane Denitz.
   Fairy dust / Jane Denitz Smith.
      p.   cm.
   Summary: Nine-year-old Ruthie is introduced to a magical
fairy world when her father hires a new baby-sitter, Alice.
   ISBN 0-06-029279-2 — ISBN 0-06-029280-6 (lib. bdg.)
   [1. Babysitters—Fiction. 2. Fairies—Fiction.] I. Title.
PZ7.S6497 Fai 2002   2001024719
[Fic]—dc21   CIP
                                                         AC

Typography by Andrea Vandergrift
1 3 5 7 9 10 8 6 4 2
❖
First Edition

For Louise.
And Mirabelle, of course.

Fairy Dust

Chapter One

Two hundred miles or two thousand miles or all the way to Mars. What difference did it make? Tomorrow morning, Ruthie Reynolds' mother was getting on an airplane and flying away.

Ruthie sat cross-legged on her mother's bed and watched as she packed. Pants were neatly folded at the crease and lowered gently into the bottom of the suitcase. Shorts came next, then the long skirt with the red and orange stripes that was Ruthie's favorite. Socks were rolled and carefully placed in a little plastic bag. Sandals and sneakers went into another bag. "Roll things, Ruthie," her mother instructed. "Then they won't wrinkle. Just because you're traveling, that's no excuse for wearing wrinkled clothing. Get me my travel bag, will you?"

Ruthie ran to the bathroom. There was the blue cosmetics bag with the gold stars that held her mother's travel supplies: Q-tips, the little orange toothbrush in its container, the collapsible cup Ruthie wasn't allowed to play with because she broke one once, a lipstick, a nail file, moisturizer, foundation, lavender shampoo, lavender conditioner, and sun block. The bag was always restocked after each trip. Ruthie used to imagine the bag had to be ready because her mother was a spy and never knew when she might have to leave in the middle of the night.

Her mother's silver bracelets clinked as she took the bag from Ruthie. "Thank you, Ruthie," she said.

"Take me with you. Please," Ruthie said. "It'll be educational."

"I can't, Sweet Pea. It's work. Someday soon I will. When you're a little bit older."

"But why didn't you tell me you were going?"

Ruthie's mother squeezed a drop of moisturizer into the palm of her hand and rubbed. "I didn't know myself until last week, Ruthie. If I'd known, I would have told you. This trip took shape very suddenly." Ruthie's mother was a professor. Last year, she went to Peru for six weeks to study ancient footwear and missed Ruthie's ninth birthday. Now she was going to

Mexico to learn about Aztec wedding rituals. Ruthie pictured her bureau crowded with trinkets from her mother's other trips. There was a ceramic mermaid from Ecuador. A patchwork purse from Peru that turned into a rat when you twisted it inside out. An Indian doll with long black braids carrying a baby in a shawl called a rebozo. "I'll miss you so much."

"Yeah." Ruthie stood on the bed and hopped up and down. "Why can't you stay home like Ellie's mother?" she asked. Ellie Birnbaum was Ruthie's best friend, ever since preschool. Her mother came to every soccer game and sometimes brought snacks for the whole team. She also helped with special class projects, like last year's unit on community, when every kid in the third grade sewed a square for the community quilt.

Ruthie's mother put her hands on her hips, staring at the two jackets draped on a chair. She chose the beige-linen one. "I have obligations, Ruthie. And please sit down. That's bad for the mattress."

"Take me with you," Ruthie said. "I don't have any obligations."

Ruthie's mother stepped closer and brushed Ruthie's bangs out of her face.

"Of course you do," she said. "Who's going to feed Tiny if you leave?" Tiny was the box turtle in Mrs. Drury's classroom. Ruthie was the only person who volunteered to feed her a handful of squirming crickets every day, even though Sarah Torrey called her a murderer.

"And Miss Miniver would be so disappointed. She was thrilled when I called."

"Miss Minivan!" Ruthie dropped to her knees and pleaded. "Not Miss Minivan! No!" Miss Minivan started taking care of Ruthie when she was in first grade. Ruthie hadn't been able to pronounce Miniver, so she had called her Miss Minivan instead, and the nickname stuck.

Of course, Miss Minivan was nice enough to Ruthie when Ruthie's father was around. Then she'd get all cozy on the couch and offer to read her any book she wanted, even if the chapters were really long. She'd also ask Ruthie to take Candy Land out of the closet, and while Ruthie was arranging the pieces, she'd reach into her brown purse with the cracked handle and take out a tin of dusty raspberry drops. Ruthie could eat as many as she wanted, even if she finished them.

But as soon as Ruthie's father left, Miss Minivan flicked on the TV and made Ruthie sit there, still as a statue, while she watched the Weather Channel. One time last year, Ruthie whispered that she didn't feel good, and Miss Minivan said "Shhh" until Ruthie finally threw up all over the gold chair. It was a good thing her father came home when he did, because otherwise Ruthie would probably have run away.

"Now stop being dramatic, Ruthie," her mother said. "Miss Miniver is lovely and responsible and can use the extra income. Besides, somebody has to keep an eye on your father. Make sure he doesn't park the car on the lawn, or stock the house with nothing but Reese's Pieces."

"I wouldn't mind that."

"I bet you wouldn't," her mother said. "Nonetheless, my dear"—she wrapped her arms around Ruthie, and Ruthie could smell her moisturizer—"this is where you need to be. Now close your eyes and hold out your hand," she said in a singsongy voice. Ruthie did as she was told, even though somewhere, deep inside, she wished her mother wouldn't talk to her like she was still a baby.

"I saved something for you, for a special occasion. One, two, three, open!" She placed a little red pouch in the palm of Ruthie's hand. Ruthie unzipped the pouch, peered inside, and turned it upside down, and a tiny gold heart fell into her palm. "I got it last year. It's an amulet."

"What's an amulet?"

"A good-luck charm. I'll buy you a chain as soon as I get home."

Ruthie tightened her fist around the heart.

"Hugs," her mother said.

Ruthie raised her arms over her head so her mother had to bend down.

"Come back as soon as you can," Ruthie whispered.

"I always do," her mother said.

Chapter Two

The first thing Ruthie Reynolds saw when she opened her eyes on Monday morning was her father standing next to her bed with his shirt half tucked in and a toothbrush stuck in his mouth.

"Ghe'up, uneee" is how the foamy words sounded. He ran to the bathroom to spit and then returned. "Get up, Sunny," he repeated. He held a fist to his lips and pretended to play a bugle reveille. "Rise, troops!" He tried to peel off her blankets. "On the floor! Attention," he said as he pulled her by the hands to a standing position.

"Go away," Ruthie said. "You are the most annoying father in the world."

"And you, Sunny"—he was the only person in the

world who called her Sunny, short for Sunshine—"are the most precious girl in the world. But I'm afraid I have some bad news."

"What?" said Ruthie. She wondered if she should tell him that he still had a little streak of toothpaste at the corner of his mouth.

"It's about Miss Miniver."

Ruthie held her breath. She didn't care for Miss Minivan, but she wouldn't want anything bad to happen to her.

"Her sister Doris broke her hip." As if he could read her mind, Ruthie's father swiped at the streak of toothpaste, and it disappeared.

Ruthie stared at him. "So what?" she said.

"So she can't come today. She has to go to Florida to help her sister. I'm very sorry for Doris, but the timing couldn't be worse." He stared at Ruthie and shook his head, as if somehow it was her fault. "Now what am I supposed to do?"

"It's a MIRACLE!" Ruthie shouted. "NO MISS MINIVAN!"

"We still need help, Sunny," he said. "I'll talk to Marion this morning." Ruthie's father was an architect. Marion was the secretary in his office. It was Marion who first suggested Miss Minivan.

"We don't need help!" Ruthie said. "We're fine."

"Says who?" said her father as he walked out of her

room. Then, as an afterthought, he added, "Get dressed. And please hurry."

Hurry. Eat your breakfast. Hurry. Don't forget your backpack. Hurry. You'll miss the school bus. Hurry. Eat supper. Hurry. It's late. Hurry. Go to bed.

"I've got to get to the office, so you can't miss the bus. Where are your clothes?" His eyes scanned the pile of laundry, slumped in a corner of the room. He scowled at the white paper, the container of water still filled with dirty brushes, and the watercolor paints on the floor, left over from last night's art project.

Ruthie knew her father was doing his best. But even though it was Monday, and her mother had only been gone since Saturday, he had already told her a million times that it wasn't easy "juggling all these balls in the air." As if it was Ruthie's fault her mother went away and he was left alone to take care of her. Juggling. She liked the idea of that: her father, dressed like a clown—maybe in oversized shoes, with a bulbous nose and a pink wig—standing in the middle of the living room with three, four, five balls spinning in an arc over his head.

Nothing was going right. At breakfast, he tried to pull her long red hair into pigtails, but they came out lopsided. The English muffin he toasted was hard as stone. She slipped on a patch of ice on the way to the bus stop, and worst of all, when she unzipped the front pocket of her backpack, she discovered that he forgot to sign her permission slip for the field trip to the bird sanctuary. This was the most special field trip of the entire year. The whole fourth grade had been preparing for this field trip for weeks. On Friday, they had cut open owl pellets and then walked down to the river to search for signs of winter-bird tracks.

"Are you sure it's not in there?" her teacher, Mrs. Drury, asked. Ruthie dumped her backpack out on the floor in front of her and sifted through the contents. "Maybe it's on my desk and I overlooked it," Mrs. Drury said, but Ruthie could have told her not to bother. She could see the permission slip now, resting against the pepper shaker on the kitchen counter.

"Well, I'm sure we'll be able to reach him," Mrs. Drury said cheerfully, as the rest of the class began to gather their notebooks and pens and put them into their backpacks so they could write down their observations. She called the principal's office from the phone in the room, and Ruthie heard her ask the secretary if she'd please take out Ruthie's file and look up her father's work number. "No big deal," she said, and then she told everybody to get on their coats and line up. Ruthie stood next to her best friend, Ellie, and waited.

Mrs. Drury dialed and talked, and when she

hung up, Ruthie could see by the look on her face that the news wasn't good.

"I'm so sorry, Ruthie," she said, and before she could even explain, Ruthie felt her nose prickle and her eyes get watery. Ellie came over and held her hand. Then Mrs. Drury softly explained that they tried to reach him at work, but apparently he had left for a lunch meeting.

"Why can't I go?" Ruthie asked.

"It's against school policy, sweetie," Mrs. Drury said. "But we'll tell you all about it. Right, class?"

Ellie gave Ruthie a hug and walked her down to Mrs. Hendricks, the school nurse. "Have a hard candy," Mrs. Hendricks said, and she reached into the glass jar on her desk. But Ruthie shook her head and pretended she was reading her library book.

Chapter Three

When Ruthie came home from school, she slammed the door to her room shut and reread the note her mother had pinned to her bulletin board before she left:

MOM'S CHECKLIST FOR RUTHIE

1. Healthy snack after school. No filling up on junk before dinner.
2. Set or clear the table.
3. Homework (in cursive, remember!) after dinner. Double-check with Dad or Miss Miniver.
4. Shower.
5. ½ hour of TV.
6. Teeth brushed.

7. Pick out tomorrow's clothes.
8. Read for 20 minutes.
9. Send me a kiss and a hug, and I'll send one too!

Why couldn't her mother be here? Nothing ever went wrong when her mother was home. Ruthie's father knocked.

"Go away," she said. "I'm mad at you."

"Come on, Sunny," he said. He tapped their secret signal on the door: two soft knocks, followed by one loud knock. They'd thought of it together, when she was only three and afraid of the dark. Three knocks. One for each member of the family.

"Go away," she said, but secretly she wanted to come out. And she was starting to feel hungry.

Her father's apologies only made it worse. "I'm sorry, Sunny. I messed up. What can I say?"

"Mommy wouldn't forget."

"Sunny, you're so tough on me." He must have been leaning against the door, because she heard a *whoosh* as he slid down. "Everything will be better when Penny comes," he said.

"Who's Penny?"

She heard a deep sigh, like when you open the nozzle on an inner tube and let out all the air. "I'm sorry, Sunny," he said. "I forgot to tell you. Penny's the lady who cleans Marion's house. She's going to help us out." Ruthie didn't say anything. He continued. "She's *very* nice and *very* responsible, and she loves kids."

"No!" Ruthie said.

"Well, she can't start until next Monday, so you have a whole week to get used to the idea." Her father spoke in that know-it-all voice that meant there was no point arguing.

Ruthie opened her door, and he tumbled into the room. "I don't want a stranger in my house," she said.

Her father sat up and leaned against the doorframe. He was wearing the faded blue baseball cap he always put on as soon as he changed out of his suit. Ruthie's mother called it a bird's nest and had tried to throw it away once, but he had dug it out of the garbage. He took it off and scratched the top of his head and said, "I forgot a client meeting today, if that makes you feel any better."

"No," said Ruthie.

She watched as he unlaced, and then removed, his black shoes with the little dots on the toes. He looked tired, she thought. The skin around his eyes was crinkly, like crumpled tissue paper. "Your socks don't match," she said, and he looked down. One was navy, and the other one was green.

"You're right," he said. "Smart girl. Just give Penny a chance. You might actually like her."

"But—"

"Case closed." He kissed the top of her head and left.

Chapter Four

During the week before Penny started, Ruthie couldn't take her regular bus home from school. Instead, she had to take the bus that stopped near her father's office. But she didn't mind. Her father looked different at work—taller and more important, sitting at his desk with his sleeves rolled up, or talking to a client. He also had a nice partner named Ray, who kept a big jar of M&M's on his desk. And Ruthie liked the way the office looked, with its tall windows and lots of plants and a miniature refrigerator that was always stocked with Diet Cokes and bottles of water.

Ruthie stepped off the bus and walked to his office, which was a long, low building at the end of the block. She opened the heavy door. Her father swiveled around in his chair, pointed to the phone cupped under his chin, and rolled his eyes. Ruthie set her backpack down in the corner and looked around. There were two long tables. One was for blueprints—these long sheets of paper with lines and numbers on them that showed what a building was going to look like from the inside. "Like a skeleton," her father always said. Once, he gave her an old blueprint he didn't need anymore. He let her fill in trees and gardens, window boxes, and a little stone path. She even drew her family, each of them waving from a different window. Ruthie thought the blueprint looked much nicer after she was through. But her father said that the design was more important. It had to come first, before any of the fancy details.

The other long table was where Ray and her father kept their models, which Ruthie was not allowed to touch. The models were made out of cardboard and looked like dollhouses, except that the parts were moveable, so you could switch things around. Maybe the staircase should be in the living room instead of the hallway. Or the deck should extend from the kitchen instead of the living room. Ruthie liked to look through the windows and imagine what it would be like to be inside that miniature house, eating a bowl of cereal at a tiny kitchen table or having a sleepover in the cozy little guest room.

"Hey, Sunny," her father said from his desk. He put

the phone back into its cradle, came over to Ruthie, and kissed the top of her head. "Nice day at the office?" he joked.

Ruthie nodded.

"What's this?" she asked. She pointed to a model of a two-story building. It looked different from a regular house. It was big and box shaped, and the front of the building was flat, with a door in the middle. And so many windows! Ruthie counted. Thirty-two windows! And each one had its own little arch over it, like a half-moon.

"You like it?" he asked. Ruthie loved it when her father asked her what she thought about one of his projects.

"It has so many windows."

"That's because it's a factory, not a house," he said. "And it's going to become an office complex."

"Oh. I remember." Ruthie had listened to her father talk about this project with her mother, right before she left. He was more excited than usual, describing how it was something different, a commercial project instead of a residential one, a real opportunity for him and Ray to spread their wings, try something new. Ruthie looked at the model again and tried to imagine window boxes under each of those rectangular holes.

Her father looked at his watch. "A quick look. I need some air. Want to take a drive and see it?"

"Okay," she said. She grabbed a handful of M&M's from Ray's desk, shoved them into her mouth, and followed her father out the door.

They drove a couple of miles, through a part of the town Ruthie had gone by a million times but didn't really know. "See the river?" he said. Ruthie saw the water running swiftly, past the garbage that had blown against the embankment. "That's what kept all these old buildings running." Ruthie looked around. "Woolen mills, tanneries, gristmills." He pulled over to the side of the road and pointed. "That was the company store, where the people who worked in the factories bought their groceries. Even kids worked in the factories. Kids your age, Sunny. Hard to believe."

"It's like a ghost town," she said as her father drove onto the road again.

"But not for long," he said. "People are recognizing the historical value and the architectural integrity of these old buildings. They're being snapped up and slated for renewal."

"Speak English," Ruthie demanded. She hated when he started using his business voice with her.

"Sorry," he said, and he pulled up in front of a large building. It looked the same as the model in his office. "This is *my* building," he said. They stepped out of the car, and she followed him as he walked around the outside of the building. "See!" he said. "Look at the roof trusses. The brickwork. Inlaid patterns around the windows. And my favorite, the wooden columns."

Ruthie looked. The paint on the two columns that stood on either side of the door had peeled long ago, but at the very top, where they met the brick, she could see the fancy scrolls—garlands of leaves—carved into the wood.

"They're Corinthian. I bet some mill girl loved to look at them every day before she had to go inside and work." He put his arm around Ruthie, and she looked up at him and smiled.

Chapter Five

Penny had hair that fell in ripples all the way to the bottom of her back. The first time Ruthie saw her, she was facing the coat closet, and Ruthie didn't see her face. Just that long hair and a little orange hairbrush with sharp plastic bristles that stuck out of the back pocket of her jeans. She looked like a teenager until she turned around, and then Ruthie saw the deep crow's-feet around her eyes. They crinkled like an accordion when she smiled.

"There's my girl," she said, pointing to Ruthie.

"Say hi to Penny," Ruthie's father said.

Ruthie waved. "Hi."

On Day Number One, Penny did everything Ruthie asked. She played Monopoly, ran after Ruthie while she rode her bike to the playground, and even gave her the answer to one of the decimal problems in her homework.

She made dinner—a hamburger-noodle casserole that Ruthie actually liked—and let Ruthie watch cartoons while she cleaned up the kitchen and packed Ruthie's lunch for the following day.

After that, the honeymoon, as her father would say, was over. "You left the house without making your bed," Penny announced, as soon as Ruthie walked in the door after school on Tuesday. Ruthie headed for the kitchen and opened the refrigerator. Penny shut it. "Not until you make your bed," she said. "Never leave a house without making a bed. It's bad luck."

"But we're not having company," Ruthie said.

"That's not the point." Penny gestured for Ruthie to follow her up the stairs. "I'll show you how to make hospital corners." Ruthie watched while Penny hoisted the corners of the mattress up and folded the sheets and blankets underneath as crisply as if they were the corners of an envelope. "Tomorrow you can try," she said. She surveyed the rest of Ruthie's room. "Put your dollies on your window seat. They can look out the window." She reached for an elephant. "Come on, help me."

"They like it on the floor," Ruthie said. "That's where they live."

Penny looked at her and shook her head. "Now

don't start being difficult," she said.

"I'm *not*." Why was it that whenever grown-ups didn't like what you were saying, they accused you of being difficult?

On Friday, Penny made Ruthie sit at the kitchen table and write her whole English composition, even though it wasn't due until Monday. "Read me what you have," she said at one point, and she put her hands in the pocket of the apron she always brought and leaned against the counter. Ruthie held up her paper and read: "'My Favorite Sport. My favorite sport is miniature golf. Last summer, my dad and mom took me to Mini Magic and bought me a sno-cone. I liked the little windmill the best. My dad got a hole-in-one at the end, which means that we got a ticket for a free game. He was lucky.'"

Ruthie looked up and waited.

Penny clapped. "Very, very good," she said. "But isn't it supposed to be three paragraphs?" She studied the assignment sheet. "That's what your teacher said. Finish it, and I'll give you a treat."

Ruthie felt like Ellie's dog, Skippy. Ellie kept a supply of dog bones in her pocket and always handed one to Skippy whenever he obeyed. She looked down at the composition and pretended to work, but instead, she just practiced writing her name in cursive, over and over again.

Chapter Six

Three days later, while the rain pounded against the windows and lentil soup was simmering on the stove, Penny and Ruthie sat side by side on the couch watching a talk show.

The title of the segment was "Help! My Daughter's Out of Control," but from what Ruthie could tell, the mother was even more out of control than her daughter. Ruthie had a hard time hearing what anybody was saying because the mother was crying. The mother said, "Sharon used to be an honors student and captain of the cheerleading squad. She was such a pretty girl. That's what hurts me the most." Penny clucked her tongue in sympathy.

Ruthie looked closely at Sharon. She didn't think

Sharon looked that bad. She wore black lipstick, and her nails were painted black. Her clothes were black too—a T-shirt, skirt, leggings, and boots. She also had so many earrings in her ears that there was hardly any skin left, and when she lifted her shirt, she showed the audience a tattoo across her stomach. It was a barbed wire fence with roses creeping out. Ruthie thought it was kind of nice, but the audience booed.

"If that were my daughter . . ." Penny began, and then she turned to Ruthie. "Do me a favor, darling, would you? Would you mind going into the kitchen and giving the soup a stir?"

Ruthie stood up and walked into the kitchen. The table was already set, and there was a salad in the middle, like a centerpiece. Ruthie stirred the soup, which was beginning to stick to the bottom. Then she grabbed a jar of peanut butter and went up to her room. She dipped her finger into the jar, pulled out a wad of peanut butter, and licked it off. She couldn't go back to Penny and the TV. She had to get out.

The rain slowed down, and she opened the double window and looked out. The days were short, and the streetlights made the wet road look shiny as a skating rink. She could hear the college bell chiming the hour.

Ruthie lifted her left leg, then her right, and kneeled on the wet roof. She crawled to the walnut tree and climbed onto a long branch, which scraped sharply against her thigh. From so far out, she could see the light of the TV flickering through the picture window.

Sharon's mother was screaming at Sharon, and the talk show host stood between them. Penny leaned forward and ran an emery board rapidly across her long red nails.

Suddenly, Ruthie felt a hand on her ankle, and she started. "What is this all about?" she heard her father ask, and she turned around.

"Nothing," said Ruthie.

"Nothing?" He set his briefcase down and crossed his arms over his chest. "That's interesting. It's late."

"No it's not, Daddy," said Ruthie. She pressed the button on her glow-in-the-dark watch. "It's only five forty-five."

"What are you doing in a tree?"

"I climbed," she said.

"And where's Penny?"

Ruthie pointed inside at Penny, who was sitting on the couch brushing her hair. But before she could say a word, Ruthie's father grabbed his briefcase. Ruthie jumped down and followed him into the house.

"You scared me," Penny said. And then she looked at Ruthie. "How'd you get wet?" she asked.

"She was outside," he said. "In the rain—"

"But—"

"Clinging precariously to a tree limb. She could've slipped and killed herself."

"I would not. I'm a good climber, Daddy. You know I am."

Penny glared at Ruthie.

Ruthie's father sent Ruthie upstairs, and she didn't argue. She spied on them from the floor grate in the guest room directly above the living room, but she couldn't hear what they were saying. She didn't come down until she heard the door slam shut.

Later, her father looked at her and shook his head. "See these gray hairs?" He pointed. "You are personally responsible for ninety-nine percent of them."

Chapter Seven

Maybe the house would have burned down or maybe it wouldn't, but it took flames licking out of the oven door to finally bring Alice Babcock to Ruthie's doorstep.

Half an hour earlier, Ruthie's father had put a frozen pizza in the oven, but he forgot to take out the little cardboard circle underneath. And now, even though he flung the smoldering pizza into the sink, thick smoke still seeped through the seams of the oven door and into the kitchen. It was the end of January, but Ruthie ran from window to window, opening them as wide as if it were a summer day. He slapped the frog-shaped oven mitt against the kitchen counter.

"That's it, Sunny," he said. "I surrender. I'll find

somebody else. Again. Somehow." He held up his hands in resignation.

"No. No more sitters."

"Sorry, Sunny."

He put his hand under her chin so there was no way she could avoid looking into his brown eyes. They always reminded Ruthie of chocolate milk. "Let's get out of here before I get into more trouble. How about Pizza Heaven?"

"Yippeee!" Ruthie said.

They stood in the waiting area until the hostess cleared a table. Ruthie was busy trying all the knobs on the dispensers, hoping a gum ball or a friendship bracelet nestled inside a plastic egg would fall out. She didn't have any luck. She was just about to sit down next to her father on the bench with the orange-rubber upholstery when she saw it: a notice written in purple glitter marker and taped to the wall. *Fun, fantastic 16-year-old*, it said. *Available after school and some evenings and weekends. Loves children!* Ruthie pulled off one of the little phone-number tabs and handed it to her father.

"Fun?" he said. "Fantastic? What about reliable? Responsible?" He carefully folded it up and aimed for the garbage. "Two points!" he said when it went in.

Ruthie tore off another one and handed it to him.

"And what am I supposed to do with this?" he asked.

"Call her. Please, Daddy! I'll call her." The hostess pointed at them, and they followed her to a booth. "Please!" They sat across from each other, and he reached for a bread stick. Ruthie grabbed it from his hand. "I won't let you eat until you do."

"All right," he said. "I'll call her. Now can I please have my bread stick back?"

But he didn't call. Not right away. Either he had work to do, or they had to clean up the house, or he was watching the news on TV. It took nearly two days of nagging before he finally dialed. He asked for references and then gave her directions to their house.

"Well?" Ruthie asked after he hung up. "What did she sound like?"

"She sounded like a sixteen-year-old girl," he said. "A sixteen-year-old girl who is going to be here in less than an hour. So could you please put your shoes where they belong, hang up your coat, and maybe run a comb through your hair so you don't scare her away before she has a chance to meet us?"

Then Alice arrived. When she stepped into the living room, the weak winter light receded. The air seemed warm, and everything was brighter, as if someone had turned on all the lamps. Alice didn't walk. She floated across the room in a pink diaphanous skirt that rustled, like it, too, wanted to join the conversation.

Her hair—so blond it was really closer to white—was pulled back into a ponytail with a pink ribbon, and it glistened. Ruthie looked more closely, and sure enough, little sparkles were sprinkled in her hair. She took off a long cape made of purple velvet. She wore a pale-blue shirt that tied at the neck and had sleeves that tapered down over her hands. And there were rings on every one of her fingers.

Alice seemed like a magical creature, someone spun from sugar and then plucked from the air. She didn't even sit like regular girls. She crouched on the floor, and kneeled in front of the coffee table, and tucked her legs under her when she sat on the couch. "Tell me what you like to do, Ruthie," Alice said. Ruthie stared at her perfect white teeth, and then at the dangling blue sea-glass earring hanging from one ear. She couldn't think of a thing to say. She shrugged her shoulders.

"Let me guess. Hmmm." Alice stared at her as if she was reading Ruthie's mind. "Art projects." Ruthie nodded. "Bike riding. Eating candy. Reading. Building tree houses. Am I close?" Ruthie nodded again. "Good! We have lots in common, don't we, Ruthie?"

Part of Ruthie resisted. "No," a little voice wanted to say. "You don't know me yet." She thought of her mother and knew she would label Alice a flake, or something like that. But instead, she found herself nodding in agreement.

Her father stood up. "Well, thank you for coming, Alice. I'll let you know what we decide."

"Fine," said Alice, as she hoisted her pale-blue backpack over her shoulders. "But let me know soon. I have another interview. Another girl." She looked at Ruthie. "Just about your age." Another girl. Ruthie felt a twinge of jealousy. For a girl she didn't even know.

"I will," Ruthie's father said. Then he noticed Alice staring at a seashell bookend on the coffee table. "It's from the Yucatán," he said. "My wife got it a couple of years ago. In a little fishing village called Celestun."

"It's beautiful," Alice said. She picked it up and turned it over before setting it back down. "Well, nice meeting you," she said.

"Likewise," said Ruthie's father. "Ruthie, see Alice to the door, will you?"

Alice opened the door and suddenly turned to Ruthie and opened her fists wide, right in front of Ruthie's face.

"What did you do?" Ruthie stepped back, startled.

"Fairy Dust," said Alice. "When you sprinkle Fairy Dust, you make magic happen."

"But I can't see it," Ruthie said. She looked closely at Alice, but Alice didn't look like she was teasing.

"That doesn't mean it's not there, Ruthie," Alice said, and then she was gone.

Ruthie shut the door, walked into the kitchen, and handed her father the phone. "Tell her she got the job. Now!" she said.

"I don't know, Sunny. She seemed odd to me."

"She's just fun, Daddy." But that really wasn't the right word. Alice was mysterious. Even a little scary. But definitely better than Penny or Miss Minivan.

"What will you do if she forgets to be here when you get home from school?"

"I'll get the spare key from the secret spot under the porch."

"What number should she call in case there's an emergency?"

"Nine-one-one."

"Maybe we should interview one other person. Just to be sure."

"No," Ruthie said. "I want Alice. Please, Daddy, please. Pretty please." She put her arms around his neck and squeezed.

"Sure. *Now* you're being nice to me." He crossed his arms over his chest and smiled in that resigned kind of way that let Ruthie know she had already won.

"Call Alice," she said.

"She couldn't possibly be home yet."

"Then leave a message."

"Can I call her references first?"

Ruthie sighed. "I guess," she said. "But then call Alice."

"Yes, ma'am." he said. He stood up straight and gave her a salute.

Chapter Eight

"**N**ow show me the septagon." Ruthie stared helplessly at the five wooden shapes lined up on her desk. She pretended to stretch her neck, but really she was spying on Marissa Pellicca, who sat across from her. She waited. Finally Marissa chose blue.

Ruthie reached for the blue shape.

"Good girl," Mrs. Drury said, and she walked down the aisle with her arms folded in front of her. Ruthie liked Mrs. Drury better than Miss Avery, her third-grade teacher. Miss Avery tried to be nice, but as the day wore on, she'd get more and more cranky. By the time they had to get their coats from the cloakroom and go to the bus, she was always sighing at everything, even if somebody dropped a book by accident.

Mrs. Drury was different. You wanted to make her happy. She never yelled, not even when she caught Shawn Michaels reading comic books during social studies. Instead, she just quietly walked by his desk and took it out of his hands. "I'll hold that for you," she whispered, and he nodded his head and said thanks.

"Octagon." This time Marissa caught Ruthie being a copycat. She glared and stretched her entire arm across the length of her desk so all her blocks were hidden. Ruthie pretended she didn't even notice and reached for her favorite in the pile, the purple one with the slanty sides.

"That's a parallelogram, Ruthie," Mrs. Drury said, reaching for the red block. "Octagons have eight sides. Think of a stop sign. You can do it. I know you can."

Yeah, right, Ruthie thought. She still had trouble telling time, and had trouble subtracting any number larger than two digits. If her mother were home, she would laugh and say, "Everybody has their talents. Not to worry."

Mrs. Drury rang a tiny bell that sounded like wind chimes, and the class looked up. "Snack time," she said. Ruthie unzipped the front pocket of her backpack, and the zipper snagged on a loose thread. She yanked again and managed to get it open halfway, just enough for her to slip her fingers in and pull out a juice box and a Baggie filled with carrot sticks.

Ruthie recognized these carrot sticks. They were the same ones from yesterday's lunch box. She could tell because she'd taken a bite out of one of them, and she could still see teeth marks. The other carrot had a black streak, where her father forgot to scrape the skin off. She didn't eat it then, and couldn't believe her father was trying to pass it off as new now. She walked over to the garbage pail and turned her plastic Baggie upside down.

Ellie held out a cupcake with pink icing and sprinkles.

"I'm quite full." She said "quite" with a British accent. This was Ellie's British year. *Quite. Rather. Lovely. Darling.* She fit these accented words into her sentences whenever she could, except around Mrs. Drury, who insisted she use her real voice. Those British words were annoying, but still, they were better than last year, when she spoke only in Pig Latin and ended each of her sentences with a snort.

Ruthie took the cupcake from Ellie and bit it in half. Ellie's mother always packed huge amounts of food because Ellie was so skinny. She tried to make the food into a game, constructing sandwiches that actually looked like Ellie, with bread that was cut into a circle, raisins as eyeballs, tomato lips, and shaved carrots that were supposed to be Ellie's curly hair. Ellie always peeled open the bread to see what was inside and closed it back again. She might tear an edge off and stick it in her mouth, but she never ate the whole thing.

"Can you come over after school?" Ruthie asked. "You have to meet Alice."

As soon as the words slipped out, Ruthie was sorry she had said them.

"Who's Alice?"

"Nobody," said Ruthie. "Nobody important."

"Then why'd you ask?" Ellie stared suspiciously at Ruthie. "Who is she?"

"Just my new baby-sitter." Ruthie tried to say this as casually as she could. Like she was talking about the new vocabulary list, or the fire safety assembly they had just had the other day.

"Oh."

It was too soon. Ruthie wasn't ready to share Alice. Alice was like a secret, a surprise, something that wouldn't be special if everybody knew about her. But she was too late.

"Is she nice?" Ellie asked.

"She's okay," Ruthie said. "My dad's the one who hired her." She had to protect Alice. Keep everyone away from her, or she'd disappear.

"Oh." It was working. Ellie was looking around the classroom, zipping her snack bag shut, putting on her coat. She was already losing interest in Alice. "I can't come over today, darling," she said, standing up. "Remember? It's Tuesday. Ballet."

Ruthie smiled. "That's okay!" she said, relieved. She had forgotten. Monday, art class. Tuesday, ballet. Wednesday, gymnastics. Thursday, soccer. It was Friday that Ellie was free. Only Friday. She'd have to remember that. It used to make her mad that Ellie was so busy, she could never make a play date, but now, Ellie's busy schedule couldn't have made her happier.

Chapter Nine

Alice was here!

Ruthie sat on the kitchen stool and ate her peanut-butter crackers. "What color is your hair?" Alice asked.

Ruthie pulled her bangs in front of her face. "Red," she said.

"And your eyes?"

"Hazel."

"Wrong. Your hair is made of midnight embers and snapdragons and the inside of an abalone shell. And your eyes are not hazel. 'Hazel' is such a boring word. Your eyes are moss and midnight ice, made from an ancient glacier."

"And what about my ugly freckles?"

"Freckles are sun kisses, silly. The more freckles you have, the more the sun loves you. See! Look at me!" Alice's skin was pale, but up close, Ruthie could see tiny dots the color of coffee milk across her nose.

Alice reached into the pocket of her pants and pulled out a little tube. "Azure glitter," she said. Then she cupped her hand and held Ruthie's face still. With her other hand, she dabbed some, cold and sticky, on each cheek. "Look at yourself," Alice said, as she held up a mirror.

At first Ruthie couldn't see anything, but then she tilted her head to one side, and the mirror image shimmered.

"You are the princess of the dewdrops," Alice said. "You better watch out, or you'll make Mirabelle jealous."

"Who's Mirabelle?" Ruthie asked. She looked at Alice and wondered if maybe, this time, she'd burst out laughing and tell Ruthie that her eyes were really green, and her hair was red, that tree trunks were not ladders to the stars, and leaves weren't kites for gnomes, and Mirabelle was just a girl she knew from school. But of course she didn't.

"Mirabelle?" she said. "I can't tell you yet. But someday, soon, I will. When you're ready. In the meantime, I have a surprise."

"What?" Ruthie loved surprises.

"I'm taking you to the Chandler Art Museum!"

"Oh." She didn't want to hurt Alice's feelings, but the art museum was the last place on earth she wanted to be. As far as she was concerned, it would be okay if she never set foot inside another museum in her life. Museums made Ruthie tired. Once, she sprawled across the smooth wooden bench in a gallery and actually fell asleep. And another time, she sneaked away from her parents and slid down a long brass stair banister. That was fun until the security guard tapped her on the shoulder and told her she'd better find her parents right away.

But of all the museums Ruthie hated, the Chandler Art Museum was Number One on her list. Every year since preschool, she'd had to take a field trip there and sit on the floor to hear some lady in a sweater talk about a painting.

"What's the matter?" Alice asked.

"Nothing," Ruthie said. "I just thought it was going to be a different kind of surprise. Can I have some more blue glitter?" she asked.

"You mean azure."

"Azure."

"Will you go with me to the museum?"

"Okay," said Ruthie.

"Then you can have more."

*　　*　　*　　*　　*

"Follow me." Alice flew up the steep granite staircase to the top floor of the museum. Her purple-velvet cape trailed behind her.

She walked so fast that every few steps Ruthie had to run a little to keep up. The museum was nearly empty, and their footsteps echoed. They turned the corner and stepped into a wood-paneled room whose walls were lined with small, dark paintings.

"Here it is," Alice said. She put her arms behind her neck and sighed with satisfaction, as if she had just eaten a delicious meal.

Ruthie looked at the painting in front of her. It was a picture of a little girl and her mother standing by a riverbank. They wore long smocked dresses and bonnets. There was a big brown basket next to them. The little girl held a pile of clothing in her arms, while the mother lifted a washed shirt halfway out of the water.

"See what it's called?" Alice asked.

Ruthie stepped toward the little plaque next to the painting. "*Washday*," she read.

"They're doing their laundry."

"If I were them, I'd use a washing machine."

"They didn't have washing machines back then," Alice said. "The working class had to do all their washing by hand. Now look close." Alice stood behind Ruthie. "What else do you see?"

"A tree."

"Look," Alice instructed. "Really look. Pretend you're inside the painting. Pretend you're standing there, right next to that girl. You're hot, and you'd rather be playing. Maybe you take your shoes off and squish your toes in the mud." Ruthie listened to Alice's voice, slow and dreamy, like she was reading from a picture book, and for a second, Ruthie really was inside the picture.

"Now take your eyes to the top of the canvas. The right-hand corner. Do you see it? Do you?"

Ruthie squinted and stepped forward. At first, all she saw was a yellow circle that looked kind of like the suns little kids drew, with rays sticking out. But then she saw it: the soft outline of transparent wings, and the body, dressed in a gown made of yellow flower petals.

"It's a fairy," Ruthie said.

"See the light, in the corner?"

Ruthie stepped closer. There, over the fairy's head, was an arc of rainbow-colored sparkles. "That's Fairy Dust. Did you know that Fairy Dust makes everything—even ugly places and mean people—beautiful?"

"No." Ruthie pointed to the Fairy Dust one more time. "I didn't see it before," she said.

Alice put her hands on Ruthie's shoulders. "That's because you didn't know how to look."

Chapter Ten

Alice took Ruthie by the hand and led her away from the soft glow of the porch light and into the dark, thick woods behind the house. The brittle stalks of dead goldenrod and milkweed snapped under their feet, and when Ruthie ran her hand across a bush of frozen red berries, they popped off and scattered in the dusty covering of snow, like sparks from a fire.

Alice held a long stick in her hand and kneeled down under the bough of a pine tree. She drew the purple-velvet cape close around her, so only her face showed. Then she leaned forward and, with a stick, drew a circle into the forest floor. "What are you making?" Ruthie asked.

"A magic circle."

"Can I play?"

"This isn't a game, Ruthie," Alice said. She made a deeper indentation into the outline of the circle with her forefinger. "This is serious. Because you know what?"

"What?"

"I know how to attract fairies."

"*Real* fairies? Yeah. Right."

"And they're here, in these woods. Who knows? Maybe *I'm* a fairy!" She spread her arms. "I wouldn't lie to you, would I?"

"No."

"But they won't come unless you believe in them. Well? Do you believe in fairies?"

Tomorrow, on the playground with Ellie, feeding Tiny, or listening to Joseph Englander belch in the lunchroom, Ruthie knew, none of this would seem real. But right now, here, with Alice, even fairies were possible.

"I do believe in fairies," Ruthie said.

"You're sure?" asked Alice. "Because they can tell if you're a liar."

"I believe in them. I believe in them. I believe in them," Ruthie repeated, and the more she said it, the more she felt them, close by, hovering in the bare branches, flitting overhead.

"Good," said Alice. She stood up, and so did

Ruthie. "Then we have to build a fairy house. It takes a special person to understand what fairies need. Everything has to be their size—"

"Like my dollhouse." Ruthie used to love her dollhouse. She even baked miniature bread and embroidered her initials on tiny dish towels. But now it sat in a corner of her bedroom, collecting dust.

"No. A dollhouse is pretend. This is real. But we can borrow from your dollhouse. Fairies appreciate real china and soft beds too, you know."

"But how do we start?"

"We start with sticks. Gather some sticks. Not too long"—she held her hands apart a few inches—"and no wider than my thumb."

Silently, they both bent down, picking up fistfuls of sticks and carrying them back to the magic circle. Then Alice showed Ruthie how to make walls, stacking the sticks four at a time and binding them tightly with dried grass. They worked for a long time, until the sky outside the woods was just as dark as the circle under the pine tree. Alice reached into her pocket and took out five sugar cubes, which she stacked in the center of the ring.

"What's that for?" Ruthie asked.

"The fairies' favorite treat, of course," Alice said. "Well, that's enough for now," she said. "A little every day until it's done. And you have to swear to keep this a secret."

"I swear," Ruthie said.

"Because otherwise the spell will be broken."

It wasn't until they stood up that Ruthie realized how cold she was. Her fingers and toes were numb, and suddenly she was hungry. "Can we go now?"

"Just one more thing," said Alice. "Spread your hands."

Ruthie did as she was told. Alice fluttered her fingers, as if feathers were falling from them. "Never forget the Fairy Dust," Alice instructed Ruthie. "That's what keeps them alive." Ruthie fluttered her fingers, too.

Chapter Eleven

Alice could recite the names of all five fairies without hesitating. "Mirabelle. Portia. Annalise. Cassandra. And Trixi, the littlest fairy sister."

"And Violet is the name of Trixi's favorite doll." Ruthie pulled the sleeves of her blue sweatshirt over her hands to warm them and then continued building a tiny stone wall.

"That's right."

The fairy house finally had a roof, made out of strips of bark peeled off a fallen log and stretched across to either side of the stick walls. They filled in the open spots with leaves and dry moss. But the sugar cubes were gone.

"Where are they?" Ruthie asked. "They disappeared."

"What do you think?"

"Did it rain? Did the rain make them melt?"

"No." Alice ran the tip of her finger over the ground where the sugar cubes had been. "Who did we leave them for?"

"The fairies."

"Then who took them?"

"The *fairies*?"

"Of course," said Alice. "The fairies."

Ruthie looked at the empty spot and grinned. "When winter is over," she said, "I want to plant a fairy garden all around the house. Each row of flowers can be a different color of the rainbow."

"Watch out, or Valentine will pick them. He never behaves when the weather turns warm. Spring fever."

"Who's Valentine?"

"Mirabelle's cousin," Alice said. "They used to play together all the time, until he broke her cloud wand." Alice reached into the pocket of her backpack and pulled out a chocolate cookie wrapped in a napkin. "Crumble it in the center of the house, near the hearth. And make sure the crumbs don't get on the floor," Alice said.

"Because fairies are tidy." Ruthie had learned a lot

about fairies in the last few days. They were picky eaters (never give them raisins, for example). They made coverlets out of pine needles but never leaves (too damp). They bathed in the early-morning dew but were allergic to rain. And they never, ever went anywhere near a spider's web.

Ruthie stood up and admired the house. The little stone fire pit held together with Krazy Glue was her idea. There was even a grate made out of paper clips, where the fairies could roast marshmallows.

"When the moon is full and our house is finished, we'll have a party for the fairies," Alice said. "Wait until you see them dance. You should see their wings in the moonlight. They're light as cotton candy and all the colors in the rainbow."

"Have you really seen a fairy?" Ruthie asked.

"Of course. Once I even saw one riding a bark sailboat down a stream."

"But how will we know they'll come?"

"When the house is finished, they won't be able to resist!"

The edge of the woods was lined with blackberry bushes. At the end of July, they were heavy with the weight of plump berries. Now their thin branches were bare and gnarled. Alice tore off a long strand and bent it back and forth until it broke in two. Then she twisted the branches into a circle until the ends met, and tied them with a leaf stem.

"You are the maiden of the fairy kingdom, and this is your crown," Alice said. "Let no one penetrate our magic circle, or contagion and death shall be their destiny!"

She stood and took Ruthie's hands and then began to chant, as they walked in a circle:

> *"Sleepy fairies close your eyes.*
> *We will guard you till you rise.*
> *Constellations, comets, moon*
> *Shall watch o'er your dream cocoon.*
> *When from your dewy bower you wake,*
> *You may nibble fairy cake."*

When they stopped, Ruthie shivered. Through the bare trees, she could see the yellow porch light.

"Now blow five kisses," Alice said. Ruthie spread out the palm of her hand and blew five kisses in the direction of the mossy bed. "And now the Fairy Dust." They both fluttered their hands over the roof of the fairy house. "Sweet fairy dreams," Ruthie whispered, and she followed Alice down the little dirt path, ducking her head every now and then to avoid the low-hanging branches she could barely see in the dark.

Chapter Twelve

"**W**alk faster," Ellie said, yanking on the back of Ruthie's ponytail. "We're going to be rather late for gym."

"Good," Ruthie said, "I *rather* hate gym."

"You hate everything," Ellie said cheerfully.

"I don't hate you," Ruthie said.

"No. But everything else."

"That's not true," Ruthie said, although her father would agree. "Don't be so negative," he always told her, whenever she turned up her nose at any of his suggestions: soccer camp, horseback riding, art class, piano lessons, acting class. She wasn't negative, exactly. Just picky. "Alice can curl her tongue and make spit bubbles."

"Gross," said Ellie.

"No, you should see her," said Ruthie. "She blows these bubbles. They're really pretty. And the fairies—"

"What fairies?" Ellie looked at her, puzzled. It was too late now, even though Alice had made her promise never to tell. "What fairies?" Ellie repeated.

Ruthie took a deep breath. "It's a secret. Promise not to tell?"

"I promise."

Just outside the gym, Ruthie bent down to tie her sneaker. "We're making a fairy house. In the woods. Want to see it?"

"I can't," said Ellie. "It's Tuesday, darling. Remember? Ballet. Maybe Mrs. Janovitz will let me pirouette on a magic carpet, and I can take lessons in outer space." Ruthie could tell by Ellie's voice that she wouldn't be a believer.

"Shut up, Ellie." Ruthie wished she hadn't said anything to Ellie about Alice, or the fairies. She'd given away the secret, and now she could never get it back.

They walked into the gym and stood in line. "I know something about Alice," Ellie said. "I heard James telling his friends." James was Ellie's oldest brother. He was fifteen and, according to Ellie, had stopped talking to her exactly sixty-eight days ago. She kept track by crossing off the days on her calendar.

"What?" said Ruthie. Her stomach tightened a little.

"He said she ate nothing but raw vegetables and sunflower seeds."

"She eats real food. She had chicken noodle soup yesterday."

"He said she starts arguments with the teacher in history class, just to get attention."

"Who cares? James is a moron," said Ruthie. She didn't want to talk about Alice anymore, not with Ellie.

"I know," said Ellie. "And he rather smells, too. My mother makes him take a shower every morning. James says Alice's mother is crazy. They had to lock her up in an insane asylum." Ellie was just making things up.

Ellie stood on her tiptoes and stretched her arms over her head.

"Twenty jumping jacks, boys and girls," Mrs. Reardon, the gym teacher, ordered. She put on a tape of jazz, and the music bounced off the high cement-block walls.

Ruthie stared at Michael Trembley, who was directly in front of her. Every time Mrs. Reardon wasn't looking, he faced his best friend, Brian Peterson, and shook his arms and legs like he had bugs crawling under his skin. It was kind of funny, except for the fact that his shirt wasn't tucked into his pants, and every time he jumped, Ruthie had to look at his back, which jiggled like pink Jell-O.

They broke up into teams and played a relay game

with a baton. Ruthie's team was winning until it was her turn and she dropped the baton. It somersaulted halfway across the wooden floor, and by the time Ruthie ran after it, the game was over.

The rest of the day wasn't much better. Instead of letting Ruthie read during Free Time, Mrs. Drury made her work with her on fractions. She couldn't find the pen her father had just bought her, and when she squeezed her juice box, grape juice squirted in her face. She studied the clock. It didn't matter. None of it really mattered. In just one hour and thirteen minutes she would be home, and Alice would be waiting for her.

Chapter Thirteen

"**W**here do you live?" Ruthie asked Alice. They were sitting cross-legged on Ruthie's bed, taking out the contents of her jewelry box piece by piece and laying them neatly on her bedspread. Ruthie lifted a top compartment and looked for her half of the Best Friends Forever charm Ellie had given her, the half that said BE FRIE FORE. Where was that charm? Ruthie looked again but couldn't find it. She was getting as bad as her father. "I want to go to *your* house."

"It's a secret place." Alice held a gold pin shaped like a pagoda against her sweater and put it gently back into its little compartment. "If I tell you, the spell will break."

"Please. Where is it?"

Alice smiled. "For me to know and you to find out."

"No fair. You know everything about me, and I don't know anything about you." Ruthie snapped the lid of the jewelry box shut and placed it in her lap. "Tell me one thing or I won't let you see any more of my jewelry."

"One thing. Hmm. My older sister Fiona is in college. She wants to be an actress. She fell in love with a guy named Jeremy. They're getting married this summer."

"Name another thing."

"Another thing. Hmm." Alice tore off a strand of Twizzler and stuffed it into her mouth. "Well, my mother is an artist."

"She is?"

"Yep. And she's moving here from California. We're going to buy a big old house and live upstairs and turn the downstairs into an art gallery. Now can I have the jewelry box?" She held out her hands.

"What's your mother look like?" Ruthie asked. It was hard to imagine Alice having a regular old mother.

"She's almost six feet tall. She used to model for *Vogue*." Ruthie looked blank and Alice continued, "That's a fashion magazine. She has long black hair and emerald eyes. My mother doesn't even have to wear makeup. That's how beautiful she is."

"So where do you live, until your mother gets here?"

Alice smiled. "Second star to the right and straight on till morning!"

"That's where Peter Pan lives!"

"Me too," said Alice.

"What about your father?"

"He got remarried. I see him on vacations. He lives in St. Croix. That's in the Virgin Islands." She snatched the jewelry box from Ruthie, opened the lid, and picked up the heart-shaped amulet, holding it between her thumb and forefinger. "This is pretty. It's so delicate." A long lock of hair, smooth and shiny as gift-wrap ribbon, fell in front of Alice's face as she studied the heart.

"My mother gave it to me." Ruthie was so close to Alice that she could smell her shampoo, spicy, like cinnamon and oranges. And then suddenly Alice was sitting up and scooping the jewelry back into the box. "Come on," she said, setting the box down on Ruthie's pillows. She slid off the bed and walked down the hall. "I want to go exploring."

She stood in the doorway of Ruthie's parents' bedroom. "This is a nice room," she said. She walked in and lifted the silver-handled hand mirror on the vanity table. "This must be really old. I love antiques."

"So does my mother," Ruthie said.

"Did she pick out the wallpaper?"

Ruthie looked at the violet pattern and nodded her head.

"Violets are my favorite flower. Did I ever tell you that? Your mother and I have a lot in common. And you know what's weird? It's almost exactly like the wallpaper in the hotel in Venice where my mother let me order *every item* on the Room Service menu."

"Everything?" Ruthie had Room Service once, in a hotel in Washington where her mother had gone to a conference. She loved the linen tablecloth, and the croissants nestled in a basket. There were four kinds of jam, and a pot of tea, a saucer with lemons, and a miniature jar of honey.

"Everything," Alice said. Then she opened the top drawer of Ruthie's mother's bureau. "It's perfect." Socks and stockings and silk scarves were neatly rolled.

"My mother puts everything away. Unlike my slobby father." She pointed to the unmade bed and the pile of clothes on his chair, with the striped sweater he wore on Monday at the bottom of the pile. It was so funny, Ruthie thought, how different he was at work, where his pencils were always sharp and his blueprints rolled into tubes and neatly labeled.

When her mother was here, she never left the house without making the bed. And the room was always peaceful and quiet. On the hottest summer afternoons, Ruthie sometimes closed the blinds, and the air in there was as cool as if the room was air-conditioned. In the winter, when it was dark by five o'clock, the soft light from her mother's desk lamp beckoned Ruthie, like a lighthouse. Ruthie liked to come in when no one was there and read through the pile of personal mail on her mother's desk. Her mother had promised Ruthie that this desk, with its drawers and neat little compartments for holding pens and paper clips, envelopes and stamps, would one day be hers.

There were two walk-in closets in the room—one for each parent. Alice opened Ruthie's mother's closet. "Wow," she said. "This is almost as big as a bedroom. Must be nice to be rich."

Rich. Ruthie didn't think they were rich. Not like people who lived in mansions, or Sarah Jennings, a girl in her grade who had an indoor swimming pool and a little barn and her own pony.

Alice studied the shoes, neatly placed in their little hanging pockets, and the purses, organized according to the time of year.

"Don't go into my father's closet," Ruthie warned. "It smells like stinky feet."

"I feel like I know her," Alice said. Then she walked over to Ruthie's father's bureau. "What's that?" she asked. She pointed to a large glass jar half full of coins that stood on a night table. It was mostly filled with pennies, but there was silver in there, too, and even a couple of dollar bills.

"My father empties his pockets out every night, and puts the change in there," Ruthie said. "At the end of the school year we do something special with the money."

"That is such a great idea," Alice said. She fingered the jar.

"Last year, we went to Ten Acres Amusement Park. They have six roller coasters. I went on all of them."

"I love roller coasters," Alice said. "Did you know that somebody went on a roller coaster for twenty-four hours straight? It's in the *Guinness Book of Records*."

"Did they throw up?" asked Ruthie.

"Don't know. Hey, Ruthie . . ." Alice tipped the jar so a few coins fell out. She turned them over in her fingers and dropped them back inside.

"What?"

"I think we should take a little of this money." Ruthie stopped breathing for a second. *Take the money?* Alice continued: "A quarter a day. He wouldn't even notice. We could make a Wish Jar."

"What's a Wish Jar?"

Alice held the jar in both hands and stared into it, as if it was a crystal ball. "A Wish Jar is a plain old jar that you make magic by decorating it, with tissue paper and sequins and feathers and glitter. I have one at home."

"I'm not allowed to take that money," Ruthie said.

"But you're not taking it for us," Alice said. Ruthie let out a sigh. "It's for *them*. The fairies. In a couple of weeks, we'd save enough money to buy them something." Alice flicked the switch on Ruthie's father's bedside lamp. "We're going to have to buy fabric to make the fairies' winter coats. They depend on us, you know. They're as real as you and me." She leaned over and lightly pinched Ruthie's wrist.

"Ouch. Why'd you do that?" Ruthie asked.

"Just checking to see if you're real," Alice said, laughing. Then she sprinkled some Fairy Dust, lifted the jar, and tipped it over until the coins fell into Ruthie's open hands.

Chapter Fourteen

It was raining hard the following afternoon, and sometimes the rain turned to pelting sleet.

"Poor fairies," Ruthie said. She looked out the window. "They don't have jackets or boots or anything. And Zephyr has a cold. How can she take care of her babies? Maybe we should bring her an umbrella." Zephyr was the mother fairy. Luckily, Ruthie had just finished putting the roof on her special room in the fairy house. At least she would be a little bit protected.

Alice stood behind Ruthie, making two thin braids on either side of Ruthie's bangs and connecting them with the butterfly clips she had brought. "Don't worry about Zephyr," she said. "Or any of the fairies. When the weather gets bad, fairies twirl their ribbon wands and make a magic halo to keep them warm and dry. There. Go look at your hair."

Ruthie walked into the bathroom and stood on the toilet so she could see in the mirror. Now her hair looked almost exactly like the picture in the book Alice showed her, which was all about the Monarch fairy. She hopped down and returned to the living room. "Don't forget Monarch's crown of orange ribbons. You have to do that, too."

Ruthie's mother only made braids and ponytails—that was all she had time for in the morning—but she always knew just how to brush the sides of Ruthie's hair together so it never hurt. She neatly tied the ends with rubber bands, and they stayed in place all day long. Ruthie felt sorry for the girls who went to school with their hair in scraggles, who probably had nobody at home who loved them enough to make their hair look nice in the morning. And even though she missed her mother, now she had Alice.

"Please! Just ribbons and then it'll be perfect!" She threw her arms around Alice and hugged her tight. Sometimes Alice returned Ruthie's hugs and sometimes she didn't. Her moods changed so quickly that it was hard to keep up.

Today, Alice pulled away. "Not now, Ruthie," she said. "I'm not in the mood." Alice retied her long, soft scarf around her neck. "Ordinary people would call this scarf blue," she told Ruthie the first time she wore it. "But we know it's periwinkle."

Now Ruthie looked at Alice's face. She didn't seem angry. She never did. But even though Alice was standing right here, she suddenly seemed far away. And then suddenly she was walking into the kitchen and washing her hands, and telling Ruthie to do the same. Her mood of a few seconds ago had blown away, like the cool air that replaces the humidity after a thunderstorm.

"Let's surprise your father!" She opened the refrigerator and took vegetables out of the bins. "Let's make a magic soup."

She opened a cupboard door and peered inside. "Carrots," she said. "Beautiful, crisp celery. An onion plump as a full moon. Potatoes. Russet and golden. And tomatoes. Fire melons." She held one up to the light. "Tomatoes are actually a fruit. Did you know that, Ruthie?"

Ruthie shook her head. Even plain old vegetables were special when Alice was around. Alice cut into an onion and showed Ruthie how, if you put a slice of bread in your mouth, the onions wouldn't make your eyes tear. She taught her how to peel carrots and slice them in long, slender sections. One by one they dropped the vegetables into olive oil, and they sizzled.

"We have to turn the heat down low, so nothing burns. And stir the onions gently, with a wooden spoon." Alice put a couple of cups of water in the pot. "And now for the final, most important ingredient of all."

"Fairy Dust!" Ruthie said, and they fluttered their hands over the open pot before putting on the lid.

Chapter Fifteen

While the soup was simmering, Alice and Ruthie transformed the kitchen into a fairy lair. They found the box with the white Christmas lights in the attic and hung one strand around the window frame. They covered the long wooden table with a white tablecloth.

"It still looks plain," Alice said. "What else does it need?" She went into the cupboard and came out holding a little container of rainbow sprinkles, the ones Ruthie and Ellie put on their ice cream cones last summer. Alice opened the lid and shook and shook until the table was covered with flecks of red, yellow, purple, and orange.

They put candles at either end of the table and then

set it with the good silver. It was Alice's idea that the plates and bowls shouldn't match. At first Ruthie thought that would look silly. But then they put everything on the table: the speckled plate under the blue willow bowl, the bowl with the rooster in the middle with the heavy white plate, the blue willow plate with a pewter bowl. It was beautiful. There was French bread carefully wrapped in a white linen napkin, so it would stay warm, and a salad. "Simple," Alice had insisted. "Just greens, and a vinaigrette."

Then Alice found some wire in the utility drawer and cut off two long pieces. She formed them into circles and showed Ruthie how to weave a crown out of the dried flowers from a vase on the mantelpiece. "Who taught you how to make these?" Ruthie asked.

"My mother," said Alice. "She can make anything beautiful." Ruthie followed her as she walked into the living room and picked up the pillows that were on the floor, patted them, and put them back on the couch. Then she sat down, her legs under her, and turned the pages of the album Ruthie's parents had started when she was little. She fingered the Mother's Day card Ruthie had made when she was in kindergarten. It was a lopsided house with a window cut out at the top. When you pulled down a flap of paper, there was a picture of Ruthie, grinning, in a plaid dress with smocking.

"That's me," said Ruthie. She covered the photo with her hands. "Don't even look at it. It's so stupid. My parents save everything!" But Alice looked closely at each page.

When Ruthie's father came home, he breathed in deeply. "Something certainly smells scrumptious." Alice looked at Ruthie and grinned. He walked into the kitchen and blinked. "Where am I?" he said. "Am I in the right house?"

Alice pulled his chair out for him. She ladled him a bowl of soup and brought it to the table.

"Delicious," he said, after his first spoonful. "Delectable. Scrumptious. Exquisite. Froomie."

"Froomie?" Alice asked.

"He made it up," Ruthie explained. "He likes to make up words."

"Tablioboocus. Reeble. Plutious."

"Daddy, for your information, you're not funny."

"Sorry, Sunny, but I'm afraid there's no word in the English language adequate enough to describe this soup."

"Tomorrow we'll make scones," said Alice. Her silver bangles jangled as she reached for the butter. "I'll bring heavy cream and jam. We'll have a real English tea. I know all about that because we lived in England when I was little."

"You did?" said Ruthie.

"Really? Where?" her father asked.

"London," Alice said. "In a flat in Kensington."

"No kidding." He looked at Ruthie. "Your mother almost took a sabbatical there once upon a time."

"Why didn't you?" Ruthie said. "Can we?"

"That was years ago," he said. "Before you were born. What brought you there?" he asked Alice.

"My father. He worked for the American embassy. More soup?" she asked.

"No thank you," he said. "But I will have more of that bread. And maybe a little salad."

Ruthie sat on a big pillow in the corner of her room and slowly tore the brown paper off the surprise package her father had handed her while they were having dessert. Everybody wanted her to open it right away, but she wanted to wait.

The corners of the box were bent after the long trip. She lifted the lid, pulled apart the white tissue paper. A little cloth girl wearing a bright poncho sat in the middle of the box. Then she read the note: *Dear Ruthie, Take good care of Marguerita until I get home. I love you sooooo much. Mommy.*

Ruthie climbed into bed and placed the doll next to her on her pillow. She burrowed under the bedspread, turned out the light, and closed her eyes. Going to sleep was like taking a trip, Ruthie's mother always said. You had to be well prepared, with all your personal and business affairs in order. That meant that lunch had to be packed. Library books and homework had to be completed, checked for accuracy, and placed neatly in the backpack. Clothing had to be laid out on the chair. And most important, all fights had to be fixed, and kisses and hugs dispensed, before the lights were turned off.

She heard the rattle of dishes being put away downstairs. Then her father was in his room, dropping coins into the glass jar. The old pipes clanked as he turned the water on, and she could hear the bureau drawers open and shut, and a click as he turned on the TV. Ruthie listened to the low voices but couldn't make out any words. She reached for the jewelry box on the night table, took out the heart-shaped amulet, and held it tight in her fist.

Chapter Sixteen

"Ruthie Reynolds, you are going to make yourself sick," Mrs. Drury said. Ruthie held the wooden spoon in her hand and looked into the little cup of chocolate-and-vanilla ice cream.

"And that's her third one, Mrs. Drury," Sarah Torrey said. She looked at Ruthie in disbelief.

"I'm hungry," Ruthie said. "Besides, it's a free country."

"A free country for pigs," Sarah Torrey said, taking a sip of orange juice.

"Ruthie," asked Mrs. Drury, "where's your sandwich?"

"I ate it," said Ruthie. "It was bologna and cheese."

"Well, that's good. Does your father know you're buying ice cream?"

"He told me I could," she said.

"But *three*?" Mrs. Drury asked.

Ruthie shrugged her shoulders. It was true that he had given her a dollar for one ice cream, but she had paid for the other two with money from her allowance. She was tempted to borrow some money from the Wish Jar and wondered if the fairies would mind. The money was adding up. At first Ruthie just took pennies, but soon she got bolder, adding nickels, dimes, and even quarters to her stockpile. Every night she made piles and counted—she already had $4.73— and then hid the money inside the Wish Jar at the back of her underwear drawer.

After lunch, Mrs. Drury told them they could work on their Valentine's Day mailboxes. Ruthie had already cut a slit into the lid of her shoe box and covered it with white construction paper. Now she was cutting out hearts: first a big red one, then a slightly smaller white one on top of it, then another red one, then a teeny tiny white one last of all.

Mrs. Drury rang the tiny glass bell she kept on her desk. Ruthie pasted one last heart onto the box and looked up. "I've put everybody's name inside my hat," Mrs. Drury said. "When I come to you, pick one name out, and no peeking! This will be the person you bring a grab bag gift for. One gift, no more than three dollars. Handmade gifts are also appreciated!"

The first person to choose was Sam Greenlaw. "No way. I refuse!" he said, and he dropped his slip of paper back into the hat.

"Sorry, Sam. No picking and choosing," Mrs. Drury said. "We are all going to be gracious givers."

When it was finally Ruthie's turn, she put her hand into the hat and felt around. She pulled out a slip and unfolded it. Matt Genovese. He was as big as a seventh grader and said stupid things in the middle of class that had nothing to do with what Mrs. Drury was talking about. Just that morning, during reading, he raised his hand and asked why the school couldn't afford to buy pencil boxes for every student. "It's not fair," he said. "Why should we have to buy our own supplies when teachers get them for free?"

"That's an interesting question, Matt," Mrs. Drury said, "and I'd be happy to answer it another time."

Matthew Genovese. What in the world would he like? She watched him lay his head on the desk and belch out loud. She was lucky. At least she had Alice to help her figure it out.

Chapter Seventeen

Sarah Torrey was giving birth. Ruthie watched, disgusted, as Claire McKenzie, a fifth grader who had a face as big and pale as a full moon, pressed her hand against Sarah's stomach and said, "Push, push! You're doing great!"

The bus lurched around a corner, and Ruthie was nearly tossed into the aisle. She looked up just in time to see Claire reach under Sarah's jacket and pull out a balled-up sweatshirt.

"It's a boy! A beautiful baby boy!" She cradled the sweatshirt in her arms. "What name do you want on his birth certificate?"

"Henry Jamison."

Samantha stood up and faced the back of the bus.

"Hey, Henry!" she shouted to the new boy with the big ears. "Sarah just gave birth to you! Congratulations!"

Why wasn't Ellie ever here? Ruthie wondered, even though she already knew the answer. Thursday. Soccer. Ellie had asked Ruthie if she wanted to play. Ruthie told her she couldn't but never told her the real reason: She had Alice. And she needed time to decorate the fairy house. So far, she had made a twig table with a birch-bark tablecloth, made chairs out of thread spools, and even hung a round mirror, which used to belong to her mother's compact, on the wall.

A paper airplane whizzed overhead from the back of the bus, and Mrs. Fermansky, the bus driver, shouted, *"You don't want to make me pull over, kids, now do you?"* Everybody was quiet for a few seconds, and then the noise started again.

Please don't pull over, Ruthie pleaded silently. *Just go.* Yesterday, when she was starting to make a milkweed cradle for the new baby, Coriander, Alice said there would be a surprise for Ruthie when she got home from school. Ruthie leaned back against the bus seat. When she closed her eyes, she could see Alice kneeling in front of the fairy house, her long, ringed fingers moving with ease in the tiny world, like she was plucking harp strings. The stick walls were securely in place, and they had put layers of moss on top for the roof. Alice peeled a strip of bark from a birch tree. Ruthie watched as she poked two holes, one in either end, and then tied a strand of grass to either end and attached the grass strands to the wall.

"What kind of surprise?" Ruthie had asked.

"I'm not telling. But first we have to buy your grab bag present."

"That's not special," Ruthie had said. "Besides, I already know what to get Matthew Genovese. I'm getting him a toilet seat. Because Mrs. Drury always has to tell him to stop the bathroom talk."

They went to the mall a new way that Ruthie had never been before, past wooden houses three stories tall, with rotting porches and old yellow newspapers piled high. Then they crossed an intersection and walked down a steep embankment to the railroad tracks. "Follow me," Alice said. "But hurry, or we'll be late."

Ruthie followed Alice up the steep, rusty steps that led to the walkway over the tracks. Alice lay on her back. "Lie down," she told Ruthie.

"But it's cold," Ruthie said.

"Hurry!" Alice grabbed her arm and yanked Ruthie down next to her.

Just then, Ruthie heard the shriek of the train whistle. She closed her eyes tight. There was a rush of wind, and finally, as the train passed beneath her, a rattling so strong, she was sure the walkway would splinter into a million pieces and she'd be left clinging to a boxcar all the way to Canada.

"Isn't that great?" Alice asked. She stood and pulled Ruthie to her feet, and they walked up the other side of the embankment.

Outside the mini mall, Ruthie fingered the five dollars her father had given her to buy Matthew Genovese's present. When she told him she was only supposed to spend three dollars, he told her to bring home the change. There were five stores: a dry cleaner's, a video rental store, a Chinese restaurant, Taskin's Drugstore, and a place called Dollar Days, where not one thing cost more than a dollar. Ruthie loved Dollar Days, even though her parents said it carried nothing but junk.

"Taskin's," Alice said, and Ruthie followed. The automatic double doors swooshed behind them. Alice walked to the bargain bins in the front of the store and sifted through the old Christmas decorations: chocolate Santa Clauses wrapped in tin foil, yellow and red and gold tinsel, and silver icicles that Ruthie's parents would never buy because they made a mess. Ruthie looked at Alice; the fluorescent light flickered and made her face look kind of blue.

"What do you want to get Matthew What's-his-name?" Alice asked.

"Genovese. Matthew Genovese. I don't know what to get him." Ruthie pictured Matthew Genovese sitting at his desk drawing monsters with blood spurting out of their mouths.

"What about a puzzle?"

"No."

"Candy."

"No candy allowed."

"I know. Follow me." They walked down an aisle filled with face creams and lotions. Alice turned around. "I love drugstores," she said. "They're my favorite place in the whole wide world."

Alice lifted the lid on a container of baby lotion and squeezed some into her hand. Then they walked past the pharmacy in the back of the store and over to the perfume aisle. Alice sprayed her wrists and neck. She even lifted her long yellow skirt and sprayed a little behind her knees. "How are you supposed to know what you like if you don't sample it?" she asked.

At the end of the aisle, they came to a plastic basket. A sign taped to it read: $$$ DRASTICALLY REDUCED. Alice picked up a small brown box and opened it.

"Smell this," she said, spraying the air. Ruthie breathed deeply and inhaled some of the cold mist. It smelled thick, like potpourri.

Alice put the bottle back in its box. "Then it's decided," she said. "He's getting Modern Spirit cologne for Valentine's Day." She looked at the price. "Three dollars. Isn't that what you're supposed to spend?"

"Yes," Ruthie said. "But perfume? He's only a kid."

"It's not perfume. It's cologne. He'll love it," Alice said. "Trust me. And that leaves two whole dollars for you. Why don't you buy yourself a present?" She picked up a set of plastic bangles and handed them to Ruthie. "Do you like these?"

"But my father only gave me money for the grab bag gift."

"Buy them," Alice said. "Tell your father you wanted to get something extra special for Matthew Genovese." They reached the cashier. "Where's your money?" she asked Ruthie.

Ruthie pulled the crumpled five dollars out of her pocket and handed the money to the cashier. The lady handed Ruthie a nickel and put the cologne and the bangles in a plastic bag.

They walked outside. Ruthie was wearing her boots, and she was glad, because the puddles were crunchy around the edges but nice and slushy in the middle.

"Ready for the surprise?" Alice asked.

The surprise. Ruthie had forgotten. "Yes!" she said, and she stood close to Alice as she opened her purse. First, Alice took out the white bag that held Matthew Genovese's present. And then she took out a box of silver icicles. "For the fairies!" she said.

Ruthie poked a hole in the box's cellophane cover and fingered the soft strands. "How'd you pay for it? I thought you didn't have any money," Ruthie said.

"I have my ways," Alice said.

And then Ruthie knew. "You took it, didn't you?" she said. "You stole it."

Alice looked at her and hesitated, but only for a second. "Of course I didn't steal it," she said. Ruthie was instantly relieved. "I don't steal. Do you know what I did?" Ruthie shook her head. "I sprinkled Fairy Dust!"

Chapter Eighteen

"It's a funny thing," Alice said, as she arranged the dollhouse tea set on the fairies' dining-room table. "My sister Fiona said that when she was in *A Midsummer Night's Dream*, some guy actually walked on-stage and pretended to be one of Titania's fairies. Fiona said she's surprised people don't do things like that all the time."

Ruthie reached inside and swept Coriander's nursery with a broom made from a stick and bristles of hay. Then she wound the cellophane icicles around a pinecone and hung it overhead. "I want to meet Fiona," Ruthie said. She also wanted to change her name to Fiona because it sounded so beautiful, just like a fairy.

"Maybe someday," said Alice.

"Tell me more about her," Ruthie said. "What does she look like?"

"She has golden curls she can twist into a bun without even using clips. She speaks French and Italian, and is learning Russian. But I don't want to talk about Fiona. What about our fairy story? They're bored, waiting for spring, and they need a little entertainment. Don't you think so?"

"Yes!"

Alice spread her cape over a tree trunk, motioned for Ruthie to sit next to her, and began:

"The Fairy Jubilee . . ."

"What's a jubilee?" Ruthie asked.

"A celebration," Alice said. "Now no more interrupting. I can't concentrate."

"When Michaela was born, her father made her a cradle out of an orange peel, and put two ribbons at either end, so the cradle could hang between the branches of the willow tree and Michaela would rock to sleep in the breeze."

"Did he sing her a lullaby?"

"Shhh.

"One day, when her mother was drying the laundry on the rosebush thorns, a tree frog leaped out of the top branch of the willow and onto the orange peel. 'Good morning,' he said in Tree Frog language. Michaela, who could speak Tree Frog, as well as every other language, answered politely: 'Hello.

Would you like to rock inside my cradle?'

"'Sure,' he said. He hopped inside the orange peel, and it smelled so good that he took one bite, then two bites, then three bites. Soon, the entire orange peel was gone, except for the little half-moon where Michaela lay.

"'And now,' the tree frog croaked, 'I shall eat you, for you look very tasty indeed!' Michaela was about to shout for her mother, who by this time had finished the laundry and was sitting on a mossy rock with a buttercup of nectar in one hand and a storybook about the land of the human boys and girls in the other. Luckily, Michaela remembered what her parents had once told her a long, long time ago, before she was born, when she was wispy idea, a wish, a hope: 'When danger strikes, be not afraid. Think thoughts of me. I'll set you free.' And no sooner did the words rush through her thoughts, like a fierce wind, than she was floating on her little half-moon orange peel, high above the tree frog, who, by now, had already lost interest in Michaela because he had spotted a very tasty centipede under an acorn. Michaela's mother happened to gaze up, and out of the corner of her eye, she saw Michaela high above her. She spread her strong wings and rose, snatching the orange peel with her long fingers and shielding Michaela inside her cloak. 'I shall never let you out of my sight again, my dearest,' she said. She put a flute to her lips and beckoned all the fairies in the forest, and they gathered. She told them about the treacherous tree frog, and they found him, sound asleep after his centipede feast, lying on his back and snoring."

Alice shut her eyes. "Don't go to sleep!" Ruthie ordered.

"I'm not. I'm thinking.

"They built a cage a thousand feet tall for him to live in and celebrated with poppy-seed cakes and honeysuckle tea. And Michaela's mother read her storybooks only when Michaela was tucked into bed, safe and sound beside her. And they never had to worry about nasty tree frogs again. The End."

She stood up. "That's it. The story's over."

"That's a perfect story," Ruthie said. "I could never make up a story like that." Alice slowly stretched her arms over her head. "Hey, Alice—"

"Yes?" Alice leaned over without bending her knees and touched the ground with the palms of her hands.

"Can we go to your house?"

"My house?"

"Yeah. I want to see the tree house you told me about. With the window boxes and the hammock your father hung in your bedroom, and your mother's painting studio. Please! We have time!"

"No, Ruthie," Alice said. She started walking briskly toward the house.

"Pretty please!"

Alice turned and faced her. "No," she said. "No. No. No. I told you a story, and that's enough. You have to know when to stop. Okay?" Each word sounded brittle, like a twig that was snapped in half.

Ruthie couldn't move. She'd stand there until morning, even if she froze.

"Ruthie?" Alice grabbed her hand. "Let's go, little fairy," she said. "Don't look so serious!"

Chapter Nineteen

Ruthie had growing legs again. That's the name she gave the pain that was sharp one minute, streamlined the next, that ran up and down her calf. The growing legs always struck in the middle of the night when she was in a deep sleep, and when she woke, it took a few minutes to figure out where the pain was coming from.

She stood up and put on the tartan bathrobe her mother had bought her. Ruthie had wanted a fuzzy pink one with matching trim, but her mother refused to buy her anything that was pink.

Then she stretched out the sore leg and massaged it. Her father would come if she called, stumbling down the hallway like a sleepwalking bear, but she didn't wake him. She wished she could sprinkle Fairy Dust and her mother would be here. Just the sound of her leather slippers on the wooden floor, swooshing like sandpaper, was usually enough to make Ruthie feel a little better.

She never stayed long, no matter how much Ruthie begged her to snuggle all night. She promised she wouldn't kick, or steal the blankets. But still, her mother waited until she was almost asleep—too drowsy to protest—and then returned to her own bed. She wished her mother were here to give her the red medicine. She loved the calm way her mother poured it onto the spoon and slid it toward her open mouth without spilling a drop. (When her father gave her medicine, it always spilled and made her hair stick to the pillowcase.) And her mother's cool, long fingers knew just where to find the pain and make it go away with a couple of firm squeezes.

She lay down and tried to sleep, but it was useless. If Alice were here, she'd know what to do. And that's when she remembered: Alice's backpack was here, in her house, at this very minute. On the floor of the coat closet. She had been in a hurry to leave and forgot to take it.

Ruthie stepped into the hallway and looked both ways, just in case her father was awake too. Then she went down the stairs, putting most of her weight on the banister so the stairs wouldn't creak. Then she opened the closet. There it was, lavender, with a rainbow appliquéd across the front. Ruthie sat down and pulled apart the Velcro. The large front pocket fell open. She peered inside but couldn't make out an address, or anything else in particular, except for some crumpled pieces of notebook paper and a math book. But it smelled like Alice—patchouli and berry lip gloss, Juicy Fruit gum and penny candy, all mixed together.

The closet was like the fairy house, cozy and dark, with its floor blanketed with coats and scarves that had fallen, and the soft tinkle of the metal hangers as they touched each other. Ruthie crawled inside and closed the door. The darkness was complete. And no more growing legs.

What was Alice doing now? she wondered. Did she sleep like regular people? Was she writing in her journal? Walking in the woods? Looking at the constellations? Or maybe Alice was floating in the air, above her head.

Chapter Twenty

Ruthie wiped her hands on her smock and stood back to admire her Valentine's Day mailbox. She had one last heart to glue, but hardly an inch of shoebox peeked through. Foil hearts and glitter hearts. Hearts strung together like paper dolls. Red and white hearts folded into an accordion so they bounced off the box like a spring.

She was a little worried when she started, because she'd used so much paste and there were sticky globs all over the box. But then Mrs. Drury came around and told her that the paste would dry and you wouldn't even know it was there. And she was right. It didn't show, except for one corner, where the cracks looked like the cracks in an old painting.

Ruthie put her mailbox on the bookcase, next to Kyle Collins'. In kindergarten, Kyle actually ate paste, until Mrs. Hendricks, the school nurse, visited the classroom and told all the kids that eating paste could make you sick. The outside of his mailbox was empty except for one huge heart on the lid, and even that one heart was lopsided. Also, he only covered one side of the box, so you could still read the words BEST FOOT FORWARD SHOE CO.

"Line up for recess," Mrs. Drury said.

Ellie walked over to Ruthie and took her hand. "Come, darling." She waved her hand in the air like a queen. "I want to get the good swings." Swings. She could make swings for the fairies. Two twigs and a leaf for the seat. And if she could make swings, then why not a bark sliding board and a tiny rope ladder?

"You go without me," Ruthie said. She had to draw the swing now, while the picture was so clear inside her head.

"Why?" said Ellie.

"I don't feel good," said Ruthie.

Ellie put her hand on Ruthie's forehead. "No fever," she said.

"That doesn't mean I'm not sick. Maybe it's something you can't see, like a stomachache."

"I guess so," Ellie said, but she looked skeptical. "I have a secret." Ellie looked around to make sure nobody was listening.

"Tell me," Ruthie said.

"It's about Alice."

"What about Alice?"

Ellie leaned close, and her curls tickled Ruthie's cheek. "James told me."

"James. Figures. I thought he wasn't talking to you."

"Well, he is now, and it's true. You don't have to believe me, but it is."

"Any day now, girls," Mrs. Drury said, pointing to her watch.

They joined the line, and Ellie whispered, "James says she tried to run away from school but the police found her two miles away, at Franklin Park."

"Yeah. Right." The line started to move.

"James said she was about to be suspended." *They're just words*, Ruthie thought, as Ellie went on and on. *Just letters, strung together like beads, and they don't mean a thing.* "James says Alice lives in a teepee in her backyard. James says Alice wore purple sneakers to gym, and the rule says you're supposed to wear white, but she does things just to get attention. James says Alice brought a box of junk from the town dump to art class so she could make a sculpture, and a dead rat fell out of a soup can." Ellie looked right into Ruthie's eyes. "You can ask him yourself if you don't believe me," she said.

"No thanks," Ruthie said. She stopped walking, and the rest of the line moved forward. After everybody was gone, she approached Mrs. Drury's desk.

"Yes, Ruthie?" Mrs. Drury took off her wire-rimmed glasses and wiped them on the hem of her skirt.

"Mrs. Drury, can I stay in for recess?"

"Why, Ruthie?" Mrs. Drury asked.

"I don't feel so good. My stomach," she said.

"Do you want to go to the nurse's office?"

"No. I just want to stay here and rest."

"Sometimes the fresh air can make you feel better," Mrs. Drury said. Ruthie didn't answer. "How is everything?" Mrs. Drury asked in a soft voice. "With your mother away and all?"

"Okay," said Ruthie.

"Maybe she can come to school and talk about her adventure when she gets back."

"I'll ask her."

"And your dad," Mrs. Drury said. "How's he managing?"

"Good."

"That's good," Mrs. Drury said.

Actually, her father didn't seem to be good. Last night, right after they finished supper—a quiche Alice made, oozing with cheese—he got a phone call from the engineer on the mill project. Ruthie could tell from the way her father spoke, in choppy little sentences, that he wasn't happy. "I see . . . You're kidding . . . What a nightmare." When he hung up, he looked at Ruthie in disbelief, shaking his head. For a second, she thought she had done something wrong. Then he told her: During demolition, they had discovered a rotten structural beam they couldn't possibly have known about. The whole budget for the job had to change, and the client was going to be furious. He talked and talked, but then he didn't want to talk about it anymore. He told her to be good and not disturb him so he could make his phone calls.

"You know, Ruthie," Mrs. Drury said, "if you find you need some quiet time and want to stay in for recess, that's okay. I think we can make an exception, given the special circumstances."

Mrs. Drury understood. How it made Ruthie tired to go outside and play with Ellie. How she had too much to think about. Alice. The fairies. School. How it was too hard, trying to fit all these pieces together, like a thousand-piece jigsaw puzzle.

Ruthie looked down at the years and years of pen marks that had been carved into her desk. Initials. Words. Some of them mean. Some of them bad. She wondered if Mrs. Drury knew they were there.

Ruthie looked at her tablet. How could she get the

fairies' slide to stay up? She drew two lines and stared. Then she looked at the face of the big round clock on the wall behind Mrs. Drury's desk. She counted the minutes. Five, ten, fifteen. In fifteen minutes everybody would come in from recess, and the Valentine's Day party would start. Last night, Ruthie had sat down at her desk and made twenty-two identical Valentines— one for everybody in her class—and a special one for Mrs. Drury, a big white heart, with a smaller pink heart inside it.

Sarah Torrey's mailbox was perfect, of course, with identical hearts on all four sides. Ruthie lifted the lid. At the bottom of the box were candy hearts with messages and little foil-wrapped hearts. She looked around. Mrs. Drury had stepped out. She unwrapped two chocolates and popped them into her mouth.

Then she stopped at Mrs. Drury's desk and picked up a picture in a little brass frame. Inside the frame was a picture of Mrs. Drury's niece, Cecilia. Ruthie knew all about her. She had a full head of hair when she was born but then it all fell out. She crawled backward instead of forward, strained carrots were her favorite vegetable, and she already knew the hand motions to "Itsy Bitsy Spider." Ruthie put down the frame and studied a neat pile of lined paper and a jar full of colored pencils. And next to the jar was a small crystal apple.

This apple was just the kind of thing the fairies would love. She could hang it from a branch, and it would glitter in the moonlight.

Ruthie waved her hands. "Fairy Dust," she whispered. She opened her hand and closed it around the apple. And then she heard laughter and turned around just as Ellie and Sarah Torrey were walking arm in arm through the door.

Chapter Twenty-one

Mrs. Drury had to ring her little bell three times before the class settled down.

"Now, boys and girls," she said, "when we're quiet, I'll let each row get up and bring their mailboxes back to their seats. And please save your cupcakes until I pour the juice. I only have one for each person." Mrs. Drury's heart-shaped earrings quivered as she spoke. "Yes, Patty?" She pointed to Patty Phillips, who was dressed from head to toe in pink. She had even face-painted pink hearts on her cheeks.

"I think it would be fair if Row Five got to go first and Row One went last for a change," she said. A chorus of "No" rose up from the Row Ones. "You know we always go last, Monica," Patty said to Monica

Smith, the new girl who wore tank tops every day, even in the winter.

"That's enough, girls," said Mrs. Drury. "You're wasting your own time. How about Row Three goes first today. And then Two, and Four, and Five and One."

"Yes, yes, yes," said Joseph Dugan, who sat in the last seat of Row Three. He made a fist and shook it in the air.

"But—" Patty began.

One by one, each row ran for their mailboxes, and then, after Mrs. Drury gave the signal, the boxes were opened.

Except for the sound of envelopes being ripped open, and occasional bursts of laughter, the room was quiet. There were a lot of Winnie-the-Poohs, and a few handmade cards. You could tell the ones from boys because mostly they didn't even bother signing their names.

Mrs. Drury jingled her bell again. "Thank you for my beautiful cards," she said. "Now are we ready to open our grab bag gifts?"

"Yes!" the class shouted in unison.

One by one, she called out everybody's name.

Ruthie waited and waited. What if her person forgot? What if she was the only kid who didn't get a present?

Matthew Genovese tossed Ruthie's gift back and forth between his hands. "Ruthie!" She stood up and got her present. It was soft and wrapped in red tissue paper. *To Ruthie from Katie,* the tag read. Ruthie looked at Katie Flynn, who was watching. She was so shy you could hardly hear her voice. She looked like a little bird and was so nice that nobody was ever mad at her.

"Okay, everybody," Mrs. Drury said. "You may open your gifts."

Ruth tore open the tissue paper, and a little ladybug with heart-shaped antennae fell into her lap. She pressed the soft fabric against her cheek and walked over to Katie.

"Thank you," she said.

"You're welcome," Katie whispered. She was staring at her gift: a skateboard key chain.

"Nice," Ruthie said, trying to make her feel better.

And then suddenly the classroom smelled like spices. Sure enough, there was Matthew Genovese spraying the cologne Ruthie had given him everywhere: on his friends' heads, inside his desk, and especially under his armpits.

Mrs. Drury's heels clicked as she hurried down the aisle and took the cologne from his hands. "Sit in the hall, Matthew," she commanded.

"Why?" he asked.

Mrs. Drury looked at him as if he was crazy. "Go!"

she said. She studied the name tag and turned to Ruthie. "Thank you, Ruthie. That was a very thoughtful gift. Everybody look around your seats and clean up, please. Then line up for dismissal."

Ruthie waited for her to open the door, but instead she rang her little bell.

"Class," she said, "has anybody seen my crystal apple?" She lifted up her assignment book and sifted through the homework bin. Ruthie held her breath and looked at Ellie, who sat with her hands folded and stared straight ahead.

"Ask Matthew," Sarah Torrey said. "He always steals my things."

Ruthie put her hand over the front pocket of her backpack as if Mrs. Drury had X-ray vision and could see right through.

Chapter Twenty-two

"My tooth is wiggly. Want to feel it?" Alice touched Ruthie's tooth—on the top, way in the back. "One more day, I bet, and the tooth fairy will come."

"The tooth fairy?" Alice laughed. "Do you still believe in the tooth fairy?" Before Ruthie could answer, Alice picked up the crystal apple on her desk. "What's this?" she asked.

"It's my grab bag prize," she said. "From the Valentine's Day party."

"Give it to the fairies!"

"I'm afraid they'll steal it."

"So what? Don't you want them to be happy?"

Ruthie stared at the apple. "Yes. But it's mine. I like it a lot."

"That's the point. You don't want to give them something you don't care about, do you?"

"No, I guess not." She opened her desk drawer and took out a skein of yellow embroidery thread, cut off a long piece, and tied it tightly around the apple's stem. Then they walked outside.

The sun felt warmer. Maybe winter was finally giving in to spring. Last night's dusting of snow had already disappeared, and the path up to the fairy house was spongy and smelled like worms and mud.

Ruthie pulled her mittens off with her teeth and placed them between her legs. Then she took the end of the piece of embroidery thread and tied it to a slender branch. The apple, though smaller than an avocado pit, was so heavy, the branch hung low and nearly touched the roof of the fairy house. Now the fairies wouldn't be able to steal it.

Ruthie lay on her stomach and reached inside the fairy nursery to replace Valentine's soggy moss carpet with a circle of bark.

Alice cleared the fire pit and filled it with tufts of brown grass. Then she reached into the front of her sweatshirt, pulled out a pack of matches, and lit one. She held the flame close to the fairy house and looked at Ruthie, smiling.

"What are you doing?" Ruthie asked.

"I'm lighting the fairies' fire pit. To keep them warm. Now the apple's glowing. See!" She began to chant:

"Fairy fire,
Burning bright.
Webs of fancy
Gossamer light."

Alice fanned the small fire so that sparks spread in front of them, fell to the ground and disappeared. "The fairies are almost ready to come," she said.

Ruthie held the heart-shaped amulet in one hand and wiggled her loose tooth with the other. When her mother was here, every night was the same: a story, a snack, water on the night table in case she woke up thirsty, one kiss, and a flick of the duck-shaped night light. Now her father did most of that—the snack and the story, anyway. (In fact, he made up his own stories, and they were usually so real—jungles and forests and gigantic rafts floating in the middle of the ocean, airplanes that took off and landed right in front of their house—that they sometimes invaded her dreams.) But not this week. This week, he was so worried about the mill that all he could do was to make sure she brushed her teeth. One quick kiss, "Good night, sleep tight, don't let the crocodiles bite," and then he was gone.

She turned her pillow over again and again, but it still felt hot and lumpy. Ruthie dreaded the moment at the end of every school day, just before they were dismissed, when Mrs. Drury made the identical announcement: "My crystal apple is still missing." Then she pointed to the tally lines on the blackboard. "Five days," she said. "It's been five whole days. Now I know it doesn't have legs. It didn't get up off my desk and walk away." That always made most of the class giggle, but never Ruthie. "It's not right to steal. Even if you think you have a reason. Class dismissed."

Ruthie closed her eyes and started counting to 100 backward. But nothing helped. She stood by the window and looked at the moonlit path up the hill to the fairy house. Where was Mirabelle? When was she coming? And why did she take away the tiny satin pillow Ruthie had put on her bed? Didn't she like it? And the picture of a basket of apples mounted on gold paper?

Ruthie pulled her sweatpants on under her nightgown and tiptoed downstairs. In the kitchen she glanced at the fluorescent glow of the digital numbers on the oven clock. She walked past the refrigerator, which hummed loudly. The dinner dishes were still in the sink, and the greasy pan that had held chicken breasts still sat on top of the stove.

She slipped on her boots and took care not to let the screen door bang shut. It was time to return the crystal apple to Mrs. Drury.

The moon skittered behind a cloud, and when it reappeared, the trees made long shadows across the lawn. Ruthie looked back at the house for a minute and then ran, fast as she could, up the hill and into the little opening in the woods. She stumbled and stood up and then she continued, barely lifting her feet, so the branches wouldn't crackle.

She reached the clearing and looked at the fairy house, bright in the moonlight. The fairies had taken the crystal apple.

Chapter Twenty-three

"Of course they hid it," Alice said, as she leaned into Ruthie's mirror and studied a blemish on her cheek.

"But why?" asked Ruthie. "Why would they want Mrs. Drury's apple?"

"*Mrs. Drury's* apple?"

"I found it on her desk, so they knew it was hers."

Alice looked at her and her eyes opened wide. "You mean you took it?"

"I sprinkled it with Fairy Dust first," Ruthie said.

Alice smiled. "Well, that's okay, then."

Ruthie frowned. "But I still don't understand why they hid it from me. I've been so nice to them."

"Hide and seek is their favorite game, you know. And they've hidden other things besides that apple." Alice counted the items on her fingers. "Your purple stamp pad. Your candy necklace. The pickle whistle I showed you from Captain Bob's Heigh Ho Restaurant. But if they took it, they must have needed it. The ways of fairies are sometimes mysterious." Alice lifted Ruthie's heart-shaped amulet out of its box. "Is this for good luck?" Ruthie nodded. Alice rubbed the heart between her fingers. "I could use some good luck. I'm failing chemistry. Did I tell you that? And it's so ridiculous, because it's not like I'll ever need to know it. Hey, did I show you my new house?"

"No."

Alice reached into her back pocket and took out a clipping from the local newspaper. "Look! There it is!" She handed the picture to Ruthie.

"I know that house!" Ruthie said. It was right around the corner from her school. It was redbrick, with an iron gate and a deep porch filled with wicker furniture. Ruthie's favorite part of the house was the French doors on the second floor that opened onto a little balcony. "Let's go see it now!" Ruthie said.

"We can't," she said. "I don't have the keys."

"When are you moving in? Can we sleep out on the balcony?"

"Oh, I don't know," Alice said.

"And we could make another fairy house there, for the fairy cousins."

"Maybe," said Alice. "We'll see." She ran her fingers around the edges of Ruthie's amulet and set it gently back in its box.

Chapter Twenty-four

Ruthie walked over to the classroom sink and turned on the water. She let it run until it was warm and then lifted the plump yellow sponge from its metal container and held it under the water until it was heavy with the weight of the water. She squeezed it and held it under again a few times, putting her face above the steamy water until the steam caught her lungs by surprise and she coughed.

Then she went to the blackboard and, starting at the top left corner, dragged the sponge carefully to the top right. By the time she lowered the sponge to the next dusty row, the blackboard above was nearly dry, and she had to rinse the chalky sponge again. Mrs. Drury would be pleased when she returned from the teachers' room, where she was photocopying some papers for their social studies unit on Japan.

Midway through washing the blackboard, Ruthie put the sponge down and shook out her arm, which ached a little. She walked over to the supply closet and quickly opened the door. In a gray box on the top shelf was a plastic bucket filled with tubes of glitter. Alice said fairies could spot glitter from a meteor away. Maybe if she sprinkled glitter on the roof of the house, the fairies would finally come, and maybe they'd return the apple. "Fairy Dust," she said, as she put a tube in her pocket. She walked out of the closet and closed the door.

"Ruthie," Mrs. Drury said, and Ruthie jumped. "Sorry. I didn't mean to scare you. Would you mind watering these poor plants for me?"

Ruthie walked to the corner of the long radiator that ran the length of the windows. Dry, warm air that smelled sweet, like the dentist's office, blew steadily. Ruthie held her hand over the stream of air as she looked out the window. If she squinted, she could just make out Ellie running to the rope ladder, which was Safety.

She filled up the watering can and watered the fern and then the daffodil bulbs that were just pushing up, and the rubber plant next to the door. It must've been about a hundred years old, with its scars and jagged edges, where pieces of leaves had snapped off. Ruthie ran her finger down one leaf and cleared away a little shiny trail where it used to be dusty. Then she wet a paper towel and polished all the leaves.

"The plant thanks you, Ruthie," Mrs. Drury said.

"It's welcome," said Ruthie. She liked pleasing Mrs. Drury.

"Not too many more days until your mom comes home, right?" Mrs. Drury asked, as she stapled papers together.

"Two weeks from Saturday," Ruthie said. "We're picking her up in the morning. We're leaving extra early so we can have breakfast at the airport. "

"How exciting."

Ruthie nodded. Ever since her father had told her when her mother was returning, Ruthie had imagined the exact moment over and over again: She'd be waiting with her father, jumping up and down so she could see over the grown-ups' heads as the passengers walked through the gate. She would hold the WELCOME HOME sign she would make high over her head, and then her mother would swoop down, like a bird with giant wings, and Ruthie wouldn't have to talk. She'd just breathe in and smell her mother's lavender perfume and hold tightly to her hand.

Mrs. Drury gave her a hug. "You're a good girl, Ruthie Reynolds," she said.

Ruthie heard the echo of footsteps on the steep stairs. She threw the dirty paper towel in the trash can, sat down at her desk, and waited for class to begin.

Chapter Twenty-five

Her father put on his raincoat. "Let's go, Sunny," he said. "Ray's probably there already, waiting for us."

"I don't want to go," she said. "It's late. I'm so tired."

"You have no choice," he said. "I can't leave you here by yourself." He looked at his watch. "Besides, it's not so late. It's only seven-thirty. It just looks late because it's so dark."

Ruthie pressed her face against the living-room window. The raindrops were huge. Then they changed to hail and bounced like tiny rubber balls across the wooden deck.

"Come on, Sunny," her father said.

She put on her yellow raincoat. She hated it

because it made her too hot. Luckily, she noticed, the sleeves were so short that she could finally put it in the Goodwill pile.

They ran to the car. Her father turned on the headlights, and the windshield wipers clicked back and forth, keeping steady time like the metronome in the music classroom. Halfway to the mill, the rain was so heavy that her father had to wait under the expressway bridge for a while until it slowed down. He put on his blinkers and pulled out onto the road.

Ruthie looked at him. He was usually so cheerful, but tonight he looked tired and worried. She had tried to make him laugh at dinner by telling him a joke. He usually liked her jokes, but not tonight. Tonight, he was too distracted to follow the story about the caveman and the UFO. It probably didn't matter anyway, because Ellie had told the joke to her a couple of days ago, and Ruthie wasn't sure she was remembering all the parts correctly anyway.

"Hey, you," he said, and he gave her a weak smile.

"Hey, you," she said.

Then they continued driving until they got to the mill. Ray was waiting in his car, reading the newspaper. He hardly said hello to Ruthie when they got out. In fact, as soon as her father got out of the car, he, too, seemed to forget about Ruthie altogether. She followed them. Ray took a key out of his pocket and turned the lock on the old door, and they walked inside. He flicked on the work lights.

The last time she had come to the mill, they hadn't been able to go in, but she had peered through the dirty windows at the small, dark rooms inside. Now it was one enormous room, and the floors had been sanded and polished, so they were the color of honey. Ruthie took off her shoes and slid across the floor.

"Don't do that," her father ordered in a sharp voice. "There's nails everywhere." Then he turned back to Ray. They were pointing. Ruthie looked up. Sure enough, she could see a crack in the beam. It didn't go all the way across, but it was big enough to see.

Her father took out a tape measure and pulled it across, from one corner of the room to another. Ray jotted down some numbers. "That's the way it has to be," Ray said.

"Right," her father said. He looked at Ruthie and pointed to the door. She stood and walked toward him, and then they both went outside. The rain had nearly stopped, and the air smelled like mud and overturned worms and spring.

"What's the matter, Daddy? Is everything going to be okay?"

Her father smiled. "They built these mills like iron," he said, "but when you have a wooden frame, something's bound to fall apart." He smiled at her. "Not to worry, Sunny," he said. "There's a solution to every problem. Sometimes you just have to be a little creative."

For a second, she wished she could tell him about the fairy house. She still hadn't figured out how to make the fairy playground work. The slide was okay, if you didn't touch it, but the bark ends of the seesaw always curled, and she couldn't get the post to stay in place without cracking. She almost told him, but then she remembered that Alice had sworn her to secrecy.

Chapter Twenty-six

*E*ven her father seemed to be falling under Alice's spell, especially after she agreed to watch Ruthie on Saturday, at the very last minute, so her father and Ray could meet the structural engineer at the mill project.

"Alice is a lifesaver," he said to Ruthie as they waited for her to arrive. Her father was whistling as he loaded the dishwasher. The crack in the beam was only superficial, hardly anything to worry about, the engineer had said, so the mill project could move forward.

He was so happy, in fact, that he probably would've agreed if Ruthie had wanted a ride to the moon, instead of the mall. Not the little mini mall where they had gone to search for Matthew Genovese's grab bag gift, but Fair Winds Mall, the real mall, with department stores and shoe stores and toy stores and a food court and ten movie theaters. Her mother hated Fair Winds. She said it had killed the downtown by sucking away all the business. She even said it was the death knell for Western civilization, which made her father laugh.

But Ruthie loved Fair Winds. And today, she was going there with Alice. They had twenty dollars to spend on lunch and a movie, and Ruthie had filled her coin purse with money from the Wish Jar. The fairies were coming, Alice told her. Maybe even that night. They had to buy tiaras to greet them, and penny candy, and as soon as they got home, they had to make sure everything was in place.

At first, they walked up and down the whole length of the mall, window-shopping. Then they went into a shoe store and Alice tried on red-suede boots. After that, she wanted to ride the mechanical cars, so they each deposited two quarters and climbed into a tiny red convertible. Alice beeped on the horn, and every-body—even the people waiting for their turns—was laughing.

Then Alice took Ruthie to the photo booth. They stepped inside and pulled the curtain shut behind them. Alice put the money in the slots, and they stared ahead. "One, two, *three!*" Alice said. She put her arms around Ruthie and made goofy faces each time the light was about to go off.

When the machine spit the photos out, Alice waved them in the air until she was sure they were dry. Then she tore the strip of photos down the middle, and gave half to Ruthie. "So we'll always remember each other," she said, and she took Ruthie's hand, like she was little. Maybe people even thought she was Alice's little sister. When Ruthie's mother took her hand, she usually tried to pull away, but with Alice, she didn't even mind.

"Want to get something to eat?" Alice asked, and Ruthie nodded. Everything smelled good—the tacos, the french fries, the pizza with so much grease that the one time her mother ordered it, she actually dabbed it with a napkin first. They walked from stand to stand, trying to decide, and finally Ruthie chose hot chocolate and chicken nuggets with french fries. Alice got a papaya smoothie.

They walked to the fountain in the center of the mall, and Ruthie spread her lunch on the fountain's wide tile wall. She opened her wallet and took out a dime. She flicked it, and it landed on the other side of the fountain.

"What'd you wish for?" Alice asked.

"If I say it, it won't come true," Ruthie said.

"We could make a wishing well for the fairies," Alice said.

"Today? When we get home?"

"Maybe. If it stops raining."

"But you said we had to finish the fairy house today. The fairies might be coming."

"Maybe." Alice looked at the clock on the wall. "If we run," she said, "we can still make the movie."

"Okay," said Ruthie.

"But . . ." Her voice dropped. Ruthie could tell she was planning, thinking, scheming. "If we go to the movies, we won't have time to do anything else. And personally, I'd rather go to Cherie's. Did you ever go there?" Ruthie had always wanted to, but her mother said it was full of nothing but junk. "You'll love it. They have everything. Hair clips, fake tattoos, key chains. Come on. I'll show you."

Inside Cherie's, the walls were covered with hair ornaments—bows, balls with smiley faces attached to elastic, clips with silk flowers. There was an inflatable yellow armchair. And tiaras. Alice placed a silver one on top of Ruthie's head. "You look like a princess," she said.

"Or a fairy," said Ruthie.

"And I want this one." Alice reached for a gold wreath entwined with cellophane hearts. They took their tiaras to the cash register, and Ruthie handed the Wish Jar coins, one by one, to the cashier. The cashier put the tiaras in a plastic bag and handed it to Ruthie.

Ruthie followed Alice out of Cherie's and into a clothing store. It smelled of incense, and the music's bass chords thumped loudly. Alice quickly pulled some shirts and skirts off the racks and laid them over her arm. "Let's try these on," she said. "We have to look beautiful when the fairies arrive."

They parted the curtains to a dressing cubicle. Ruthie sat on the floor and looked at herself in the three-way mirror. "What do you think?" Alice asked. The skirt was sky blue, with tiny gold bells sewn into the fringes on the bottom.

"Good." *You look perfect in anything,* Ruthie thought. "Are you going to get it?"

"I think the fairies would approve, don't you?" Alice stepped out of the skirt, rolled it into a tight ball, and stuffed it into her backpack. "Your turn," she said. "Here." She handed Ruthie a silky green shirt that tied at the waist.

"This is for grown-ups," Ruthie said.

"Just try." Ruthie took off her sweatshirt, and Alice guided her arms through the shirtsleeves. It was light and filmy, more like air than cloth. "Now look at me," Alice said. She took a lipstick out of her purse and put some on Ruthie's mouth. "See. This is what you're going to look like in five years. Okay," she said. "Let's go. I think the fairies will be happy with us." Ruthie started to take the shirt off, but Alice stopped her. "Put your sweatshirt over it," she whispered. "Nobody will ever know."

Stealing. Alice wanted her to steal.

"But we shouldn't," Ruthie said.

Alice looked annoyed. "They're sale clothes. They want to get rid of them, believe me."

"But—"

Alice was insistent. "Sprinkle it with Fairy Dust!" Her fingers fluttered close to Ruthie's chest. "Hurry," Alice said. She handed Ruthie her sweatshirt, and Ruthie put it back on.

Then Alice slipped her backpack over her shoulder and took Ruthie's hand. She parted the curtain, smiled at the sales clerk, and paused to study a pair of dangly earrings. She ran her hand across some red-velvet pants. She smoothed the ribbon around a stuffed teddy bear's neck. She opened a pot of crème de menthe lip gloss and inhaled deeply. And then they stepped out of the store.

A high-pitched shriek. Static from walkie-talkies. Ruthie looked at Alice. What was happening? Why wasn't Alice saying anything? Alice didn't move.

"Alice," Ruthie said. "Alice, what's that noise?"

"Shut up, Ruthie, " Alice said, without looking at her. "Just shut up."

A big lady in a uniform took them both by the arms and quietly led them away.

Chapter Twenty-seven

Ruthie waited three whole days before she even mentioned Alice's name. "Surely you jest," Ruthie's father said, and he leaned so far back in the kitchen chair that Ruthie thought he was going to tip backward. "You're dreaming, Sunny."

"I am not dreaming," Ruthie said. "And I do not give you permission to fire Alice. Don't you care what I think? Don't I have any say in this at all? Mommy wouldn't let you fire her."

"Mommy isn't here," her father replied. "When Mommy is here, then Mommy will be part of the discussion."

"I don't like you!"

"And I don't like baby-sitters who are thieves. And

make my child their accomplice."

"She's not a thief."

"No. She's just a lovely young lady who steals from department stores."

"She said she wouldn't do it again."

"No, thank you," said her father. "I prefer not to have a replay of that afternoon."

Ruthie could still picture the lady—a security guard—leading them down a long corridor until they reached a cubicle that was not much bigger than the dressing room. The security guard asked Alice if she could see her purse.

At first Alice told her no, that it was an invasion of privacy.

But then the guard said she didn't really have a choice, so Alice practically threw it at her. "Go ahead; there's nothing in there," she said. She dumped the contents of her makeup bag on a little table, and Ruthie caught a clear tube of white lipstick just before it hit the floor. The guard held out her hand, and Ruthie gave it to her.

"That's mine," Alice said. The guard examined it and put it back on the table.

"And what's in that bag?"

"We paid for it," Alice said. She waved the tiaras in the air and then showed her the receipt.

"Your address and phone number?" She stood over

Alice like a giant, with her feet apart and her arms crossed over her chest.

Alice shook her head. "I don't have to tell you."

"Oh yes you do. Your address and phone number," she repeated.

Ruthie waited. Alice hunched down in the metal chair. She had pulled the sleeves of her shirt over her hands, and her purple-velvet cape covered all of her so that only her head showed. Ruthie thought she looked small, even smaller than her. "One thirty-three Haley Street," Alice whispered. And then she recited her phone number in a flat voice.

"Thank you," said the guard as she wrote it down. "And what else do you have to show me, girls?"

Ruthie didn't know what to say. She felt like if she sat there long enough, she might turn into an ice sculpture, or a piece of petrified wood like the one Mrs. Drury once showed the class. Maybe the guard, and Alice, too, would turn into petrified wood, and they'd never have to speak or move again.

"Nothing," said Alice.

"Yeah, right," the guard said. "That's not what the salesgirl told me. Why don't you both take a little walk to the bathroom right there and gather whatever doesn't belong to you."

Alice and Ruthie walked silently to the bathroom. Ruthie looked at Alice and waited for her to say something, but Alice stared at the floor. Ruthie took off the silky green shirt, and Alice took the sky-blue skirt out of her backpack. They walked back to the guard's cubicle and placed the clothes on the little table.

"Is this your little sister?" the guard asked Alice.

"No. I'm just her baby-sitter."

"Well, shame on you," she said to Alice. Then she dialed the phone number Alice gave her, but there was no answer.

"What's your phone number?" the guard asked Ruthie.

"Nobody's home," Ruthie said. "My father's at work."

"Where's he work?"

Ruthie told her the name of the architectural firm. The guard looked it up in a phone book and dialed.

While the guard waited, she tapped her thick fingers on the table, one after the other, like a drumroll. Finally, she said "Hello." But she turned her back, and Ruthie couldn't hear anything else she said. Then the guard hung up. "He's on his way," she said.

Ruthie stared at the clock. It took her father exactly thirty-three minutes to arrive. He was polite to the guard and shook his head sadly at Ruthie and then Alice.

"I'll take you home," he said to Alice, after they walked out to the car. "You're lucky you only got a warning. She could have pressed charges. So tell me your address."

"I'll walk from your house," Alice said. "I have to get my bike."

"But it's raining. The roads are slippery. Your mother wouldn't want you to ride," he said.

"My mother wouldn't care."

"But—"

"Just let me get my bike. Please."

When they got back home, the rain was coming down even harder. Alice opened the car door and stepped out. She lifted the hood of her cape over her head and dashed toward her bike, which was resting against the garage door. Ruthie followed her.

Alice spread her cape out in front of her. Then she pulled it over her head. "I might as well throw it away. It's ruined," Alice said.

"Don't throw it away! You said it was magic!"

"If you like it so much, then you take it," Alice said, and she tossed the cape onto the sidewalk.

"What about the fairy house? We have to finish it. What if they come tonight?"

"Ruthie!" her father called. The front porch light turned on, and she saw him standing in the doorway.

"We have to set the table for the feast. You said they wouldn't wait."

"Ruthie!" he called again. "Come in right now!

You're going to catch a cold!"

"What should I do? Tell me what to do!" She held on tight onto Alice's bike seat.

Alice pushed her hand away. "You figure it out. I have to go," she said, and she rode away.

Chapter Twenty-eight

Ruthie sat down and stared at the plate her father set in front of her. "You mixed it," she said.

His spoon stopped in midair. "What are you talking about?"

She pushed the plate away and pointed. "The applesauce is touching the grilled cheese."

"So?"

"That's what the cafeteria ladies do. It's repulsive. Alice never mixes my food."

"I know you are going to miss Alice, aren't you, Sunny?" He tore his grilled cheese in two and dipped a corner of it in ketchup.

"You're mean," Ruthie said.

"No I'm not. Sunny, your friend Alice is a troubled

girl. She needs help." He shook his head. "And frankly, I would have thought you had better judgment. What were *you* thinking, walking out of a store wearing clothes that didn't belong to you? And not going to the movies like you said you would?"

"We changed our minds. Call her, Daddy, please! Just give her one more chance!"

"I'm sorry, Sunny. My heart goes out to Alice. It really does." For a second, Ruthie was hopeful. "But it's you I care about. Your happiness—"

"I *was* happy."

"And more importantly, your safety. You need to be with somebody I can trust." Ruthie knew there was no longer any hope of getting Alice back. She looked at her father and started to cry. "I'm so sorry, Sunny," he repeated. "I know how much you loved her. And she loved you, too. But she's fired. That's the way it has to be. Period. Finis."

"If I make a mistake, are you going to fire me? I thought you said we all learn from our mistakes," Ruthie said.

"You're my daughter, Sunny," he said. His face softened. "I wouldn't fire my own daughter." He peeled open his grilled cheese sandwich and squeezed ketchup inside. "Alice is not my daughter. I can't be responsible for her behavior. Only yours."

"I wish you weren't my father," Ruthie said, and

even though her head was down, she raised her eyes a little bit to look at him. He was smiling a little, which only made her madder. "I wish I had a different father. Maybe I'll run away."

"If you're going to run away, then you're going to need your allowance," he said.

"I'm not joking!" Ruthie said, standing up. "Stop treating me like a baby!"

He reached into his pocket. "I don't know what happened to all my change. I thought I had more change in that jar . . ."

Ruthie stood still.

". . . You know, the one on my dresser. It's mostly bills now. And pennies. I could swear I had more silver. Maybe Alice has been in there, too."

"She has not," Ruthie said. "You always have pennies. You have no memory."

"You're right about that," he said.

"Mommy remembers everything."

He handed her some coins.

Ruthie stared at them. "I don't want my allowance." She hurled the coins into the living room, and they scattered—into the fireplace, under the couch, behind the bookshelf. Then she ran and opened the front door.

"Close that door, Sunny. It's raining."

"Make me," she said as she started to step outside.

"Come on, Sunny, I'm too tired to play games."

Ruthie spun around and spit the words out, like little flecks of hail: "My name's not Sunny, it's *Ruthie*." She put on Alice's purple cape and ran all the way to the fairy house.

In the magic circle under the pine bower, the fairy house was protected. Not even the worst snowstorm of the season damaged it, unless you counted a tiny snow-drift against the fairy pantry. Ruthie had to work quickly, before her father came looking for her. It was hard to believe that only four days earlier she and Alice had chosen their menu for the fairy banquet: fairy nectar, blossom salad, and sweet drops. Behind a large boulder, protected from the wind and wrapped in a plastic bag, was everything she and Alice had already gathered.

She took the piece of handkerchief she had cut into a circle and laid it on the dining-room table. First she set the table with seven acorn cups—one for each of the fairy sisters, and one each for Alice and herself, as well. Next to each cup she placed a little tuft of cotton ball for a napkin, and she set out seven plates she'd taken from her dollhouse. Four of them were blue-flecked enamel, and the other three were white, with pink carnations. She poured fairy nectar—sugar water—from a water bottle. On one birch-bark platter she arranged the blossom salad—wild berries, dried flower petals from a potpourri sachet in the back of Ruthie's mother's underwear drawer, and green grapes, cut up into morsels no bigger than a seed bead. And on the other birch-bark platter she placed chocolate chip drops and sugar roses and chocolate leaves.

"How will I know if they're coming?" Ruthie had asked Alice.

"You'll know," said Alice. "They always give a sign when they know the coast is clear."

Ruthie fluffed up the five milkweed comforters on the five twig beds—or three twig beds, because they had borrowed a bunk bed from the dollhouse. She snapped off some kindling and placed it neatly in the center of the tiny fire pit. As soon as she went inside, she'd get the kitchen matches, hidden high in the cupboard over the stove. Then she could come back and light a fire for the fairies. They'd be happy to have a place to warm their tired wings, which were always heavier in the winter, when they had to flutter them almost all the time, so the icy air wouldn't cause them to freeze.

Softly, she recited the poem she had memorized the other day:

> *"Welcome, come,*
> *Dear fairy friends.*
> *Enjoy this feast*
> *Till winter ends.*

In silver rain
Or sunbeam skies,
We hope this home
Delights your eyes."

The circle was friendly. It was safe to come out.

"Ruthie!" Her father's voice called, sudden and sharp in the night air. "Ruthie!"

She had to protect the fairies. It wasn't time. Not yet. She ran back down the hill toward her house.

Chapter Twenty-nine

After school the next day, Ruthie pulled her beret over her ears, hopped on her bike, and began pedaling. Silently, she chanted the street address Alice had given the guard at the mall after they got caught. 133 Haley Street. 133 Haley Street. New Hartford. Plymouth. Lincoln. Castle Way. Ruthie mouthed the names to herself as the street signs flew past. Summit. *Haley.* She made a right turn and began to count: 13, 15, 17, 19, 21.

Alice's house would be easy to find. She looked for it, gray-blue with a wraparound porch, and a turret like Rapunzel's on the top: 57, 65, 81. Ruthie navigated over a pothole and watched the numbers closely: 133. *133.* How could this be it? It was so small. Two stories high, but the shape of a box. It had red-aluminum siding, and peeling paint around the window frames, and a black railing next to cement steps that were chipped and cracked.

Maybe there was a mistake. Maybe this was Alice's mother's studio, and her house was the one in the picture in the paper. She pressed the doorbell, and nothing happened. But then a sound like church bells pealed inside the house. There were footsteps, and the door opened. A lady with gray hair answered the door. "Well hello," she said. "Can I help you?"

This couldn't be Alice's mother. Maybe she was the housecleaner. Or the cook. "I'm Ruthie," she said.

"Ruthie! I'm Alice's grandmother."

Alice's grandmother.

"Alice!" she called. "So you're Ruthie," she said, and she shook her head and smiled.

Ruthie looked up at the top of the staircase.

"Hi, Ruthie," Alice said. Alice's hair was wet and hung straight and long, past her shoulders. She was wearing a red-and-blue kimono with a dragon embroidered on it. Her feet were bare, and her toenails were painted blue. Ruthie remembered all the things she had stored up to tell Alice: Mrs. Drury cut her finger slicing carrots for a salad and had to have five stitches. Ellie didn't sit with her on the bus anymore. Her mother was coming home. "How did you know where I was?" she asked as she motioned for Ruthie to climb the stairs.

You gave the guard at the mall your address. Ruthie hesitated. Did Alice's grandmother know about what had happened?

"I looked in the telephone book," Ruthie said.

Alice walked down a hallway. "Sorry about what happened," she said. "I didn't mean to get you into trouble." She walked into a room.

Was this Alice's room? Ruthie looked around. What happened to the hammock? And where were the little white lights around the windows? And the fairy mural her mother painted on the wall? Instead, there was a plain brown desk and a matching brown bureau, and an oval hooked rug between two twin beds. The lamp on the night table had a pink crinoline shade that looked like a hoop skirt. Ruthie sat on the edge of one of the beds, careful not to upset the row of stuffed animals behind her.

Alice leaned against a pillow on the other bed. "So what's new, Ruthie?" she asked.

Ruthie was just about to tell Alice all about how she had finished the fairy house, and the fairy fruit salad, when she saw it: There, on the windowsill, was a little crystal apple, just like the one Ruthie took from Mrs. Drury's desk. She leaned closer and studied it.

"That's just like our apple, isn't it?" Ruthie said.

Alice turned to look. "Is it? I've seen hundreds of them. My grandmother got that for me at a tag sale."

"But our apple's missing."

"Is your mother back yet?"

"No," said Ruthie. "Not yet."

Alice looked in the mirror and put on red lipstick and mascara. She took a hairbrush off her dresser and leaned over and brushed.

And then Ruthie saw something else: the heart-shaped amulet, dangling from a thin gold chain around Alice's neck. Ruthie froze.

Alice continued brushing. *You said the color of your walls was hydrangea,* Ruthie thought. *These walls are green. Pukey hospital green.* "That's too bad, your mother's not home yet," Alice said. "I mean, she's always gone, isn't she?" *And you said there was a little balcony outside your window.* Alice stretched her arms over her head, and the amulet danced back and forth. *You said you had a patchwork quilt just like mine on your bed, but I don't see a quilt.* "If I were you, I'd be really mad." The necklace spun backward, so its smooth side showed.

Ruthie sat still. "What?" said Alice. "What are you looking at?"

Ruthie walked over to Alice. Away from Ruthie's house, under the bare overhead lightbulb you had to yank on with a string, Alice looked different. Ruthie tried but couldn't see any glitter. Alice's skin was pale, like she needed to get some fresh air, and there was even a red splotch on her chin. Ruthie took a deep breath. "Is that my necklace?" she asked.

"You're crazy. My mother got it for me, for my birthday. Besides, yours didn't have a chain, did it?"

"It looks just like mine."

"What?" Alice smiled a slow, relaxed smile and stretched out, like she had all the time in the world, like they were talking about something nice, like fairy menus. "They're not that hard to find, Ruthie. Besides, doesn't yours have a little heart inside the big heart?" Ruthie tried to remember. "See." She pointed to Ruthie, who came closer. "Mine doesn't."

"Alice!" The grandmother's voice carried down the carpeted hallway. "Time to get dressed. We have to go to the market!"

"Where's your mother? I want to meet her," Ruthie demanded.

"I live with my grandmother, Ruthie. I already told you that."

"You did?" *I don't remember.* "And her house, and her art gallery, and Fiona. Show me your house. I thought you had a nice house."

"Alice!"

"I'm coming, Gran!"

"Tell me!"

"Oh. Are you my boss?" Alice asked. She stood up and put on her shoes. "And speaking of bosses, Ruthie, your father still owes me twenty bucks. Could you tell him I need it?"

"Fiona. When can I meet her?"

"Go away, Ruthie! Stop bothering me!" Alice walked toward the door.

Ruthie slammed it shut. She was crying now. "Are you going to come back when the fairies arrive?"

Alice put her hands on her hips and stared at Ruthie. "Aren't you a little old for fairies?"

"The fairies were your idea."

"Well, they were a stupid idea. Go away, Ruthie. Go home." Alice gripped Ruthie's shoulder so hard it hurt. Then she loosened her fingers, grabbed the doorknob, and opened the door.

"Where's the hammock? Where's your mother?"

"I can't stand you!" Alice screamed. "You're always bugging me about my mother."

"But you said—"

"Why do you care so much about my mother? Why can't you leave me alone!"

"I'm sorry. You told me she was coming. I wanted to meet her. I was just being nice." The words came out jagged, between sobs.

"You want to know where she is?" Alice screamed. "I'll tell you where she is." She leaned close and whispered. "I found a note last spring. Right after I came downstairs for breakfast. I found a note on the kitchen counter. Leaning against my bottle of vitamins. She said she needed a change. The note said she'd call me that night. She didn't call me, by the way. And guess what? Now she's living in California with my lovely new stepfather. And his lovely daughters. Okay, Ruthie? That's where she is. And if she thinks I'm coming—"

Alice's bedroom door opened, and her grand-mother stepped in. "So much noise," she said. She looked at Alice and walked over to her quickly. Alice was shaking her fist in the air. She took Alice's fist in her own hand and led her to the bed. They sat down, and she put her arm around Alice.

Ruthie stood still until the grandmother looked at her. "I think you'd better go now, dear," Alice's grand-mother said. "It's been a long day."

Ruthie walked over to the windowsill and lifted up the crystal apple. "This is not yours. It belongs to the fairies," she said, and she ran out of Alice's room and down the stairs.

Chapter Thirty

Ruthie's bike nearly crashed when she rode over a log that had fallen and was lying in the middle of the road. It was dark now, and hard to see. She breathed so hard that the rushing noise inside her head sounded like a seashell against her ear. She hopped off her bike and didn't even bother with the kickstand; the bike fell to the ground.

She ran upstairs and reached for her jewelry box. She opened the lid. Everything was exactly where it belonged. Her rings were on the left side of the little tray, and the charm bracelet her parents gave her for her eighth birthday was on the right. When she lifted the tray, she saw the necklaces Alice had untangled, lying side by side on the bottom. And next to them were several pins. But just as she already knew, the heart-shaped amulet was gone.

"Ru-thie!" her father called from inside the house. He must have heard her come in. "Where are you?"

Good, Ruthie thought. A screen door slammed, and she heard his footsteps on the porch below. "Ruthie!" he called in every direction.

Ruthie filled a blanket with all the presents her mother had ever given her: masks and carved wooden animals, Indian girls with long black braids, woven sandals, beaded jewelry, hair clips, books, face paint, worry dolls, embroidered dresses, a tortilla press. She gathered them tightly and ran to her parents' room and deposited all the presents on her mother's side of the bed. Why wasn't she here to make everything all right?

Back in her room, Ruthie carefully opened her window wide and looked below. The porch light had been flicked on, and she could see the top of her father's baseball hat, which was tipped to the side so that a little bit of balding head showed under his thinning hair. He stood in the center of the porch and turned around.

A branch snapped. Maybe it was a coyote. She had heard them before, wailing in the middle of the night. It must have reached the mossy grass of the open meadow. Her father walked to the edge of the porch, to the railing, and leaned out, listening. Beyond the porch and just inside the woods was the fairy house. Another branch snapped. The fairies. Who was going to protect the fairies? Who was going to tell them that it was safe to come out?

Ruthie tiptoed down the stairs, carrying the matches she had taken from the kitchen, and went out the front door, up the hill, and into the woods.

She fingered the fairy house's sturdy walls. The birch bark platters were just where she'd left them. Except for a few loose patches, the moss roof was still in place. Zephyr's room was tidy. Ruthie fingered the vine hula hoops in the nursery. She had made them for the five fairy sisters. Each little room was now complete, cozy but sturdy, the way she had always hoped they would one day be. The fairy house shimmered under the full moon. Ruthie widened the fire pit and added thicker branches to the pile of twigs. Now the circle was enchanted. It was time for the fairies to appear.

She lit a match and held it out, like it was a magic wand. The little flame touched the kindling. The wood was damp, and a gray funnel of smoke extended upward and then evaporated. And then there was a wind. The fire pit burst into flame, and the flames reached in all directions. Ruthie walked around and around the fire pit, chanting:

"Deep beneath the darkest hour,
See, dear fairies,
Our fire shower.
Join our circle,
Hear our song.
The day's far off,
Sweet night is long."

The wind died down. She fanned the flame with her hands, and sparks flew. The sparks had to be a sign that the fairies were coming. *Please come. Now. I'm waiting.* Another swirl of the stick. But when? When would they appear? Ruthie kicked the fire pit with the tip of her toe. The sparks flew again, higher this time.

An ember fell on Zephyr's mossy roof. The roof sizzled, then burst into flames. The flames spread to the five fairy sisters' bedroom, and Coriander's nursery. *Maybe you're not coming. Maybe you* never *were going to come. Did you trick me?* Ruthie wondered. And then, a horrible thought. *Alice lied about her mother. She lied about her sister. She lied about everything. The fairies weren't real. And neither is Alice.* The fairy playground burned. The kitchen. Higher and higher. Beyond the magic circle. The fairy house was disappearing.

A sound. Footsteps. Rhythmic and strong. The smell of wet wool. And then her father's voice:

"Ruthie, what the hell do you think you're doing?" She didn't look at his face—just his big black shoes stomping on the flames. "Well? What is this all about?"

"Nothing," she said.

"Nothing!?" He threw some damp leaves on top, and the smothered flames turned to smoke. "Tell me. Who gave you permission to play with fire? Was that the wonderful Alice's influence?"

Ruthie picked up the little blue-enamel pot and put it in her pocket. "It's my fairy house. I can do anything I want to it!"

"What are you talking about?"

"The fairies aren't coming."

"The fairies?" Ruthie's father held out his hand. "Give me the matches." She handed them to him. "What ridiculous ideas has Alice been putting into your head?"

"I don't want to talk about them anymore. They're not coming. I hate them!" Ruthie stood up. She was shaking. The sky and the clouds and the branches spun like a kaleidoscope. She ran down the dirt path. She could hear her father following; a branch cracked, and he cursed. He must have stumbled, but now she could hear him running again.

"Ruthie! Stop!" he shouted. "I can't keep up with you."

But Ruthie didn't stop until she reached the open meadow. She was crying and hiccuping at the same time. She curled up in a ball in the tall grass and put her hands over her head. Her amulet was gone. The fairy house was gone. Alice. Everything.

"Is it time for your mother to come home?" Her father was here. He kneeled behind her and put his hands on her shoulders. "I think it's time. What do you think?"

"I don't care," Ruthie said in a small voice.

"*I* care," said her father. "I think she's been gone long enough, thank you." His voice was fiercer now, as if he were talking to Ruthie's mother, and not to Ruthie. "Don't you agree?"

Ruthie nodded her head. "Yes."

They sat there saying nothing until Ruthie's foot fell asleep. And then she spoke. "Daddy," she said, "I have something to tell you."

"Anything," he said. "Anything at all." And she told him, in one long sentence, without stopping, all about Alice and the Fairy Dust and the Wish Jar and the coins she took. And with every thing she told him, she felt lighter.

"I'm sorry," she said. Ruthie wasn't angry anymore. Just tired and kind of wilted, like a puckered old helium balloon that had lost most of its air.

"You're forgiven." They began to walk back. Her father stopped as they passed the remains of the fairy house. "You know," he said, "you can always start over.

Sometimes, when you start over, it's even better than the first time around."

"Maybe," Ruthie said. "I don't know. Maybe."

"And you know what?" he said.

"What?"

He pulled her close. His sweater was scratchy, but she didn't mind. "There's still Fairy Dust here, Sunny," he said. "I'm sure there is."

Chapter Thirty-one

Ruthie was waiting all day for the right moment to return the crystal apple to Mrs. Drury's desk. She was going to do it just before they went to the library, and then on their way to recess, but both times, Mrs. Drury was sitting there, correcting homework papers.

Part of Ruthie wanted to keep the apple. She was sure Mrs. Drury didn't suspect her—she'd pick one of the boys first, like Michael Trembley, whom she once caught in the supply closet stealing an eraser. But the other part of her wanted to get rid of it, like it had cooties, or the plague.

Her hand was sweaty from holding it so tight all morning, and the tape that was holding the tiny note that said *Sorry* was starting to peel. It was quiet reading time. Mrs. Drury was over by the windowsill, watering the sunflower seeds they'd stuck inside paper cups first thing that morning. Ruthie put her book down and walked up the aisle toward Mrs. Drury's desk. She had a pencil in her hand that didn't really need to be sharpened, but she carried it just in case somebody asked her what she was doing. In one smooth movement, she raised her arm and released the apple gently, next to Mrs. Drury's coffee mug. Then she sharpened her pencil and sat down.

Mrs. Drury didn't see the apple until the very end of the day. She picked it up and read the note. Then she rang her little bell, and the class quieted down. "I'd like to say 'Thank you' to the person who returned my apple. I'm proud of you for changing your mind and deciding to return it."

Ruthie turned to look at Ellie, and Ellie was looking right at her, and she was smiling.

The night before the morning they drove to the airport to pick up Ruthie's mother, Ruthie called Ellie and asked if she wanted to help her make a WELCOME HOME banner to hang across the front door. She had missed Ellie. Ellie made each letter a different color, and outlined the letters in black, so they stood out. Then she used up a red-yellow-and-silver glitter glue, drawing pictures of hearts, moons, and flowers all around the border of the paper. Ruthie was going to add a fairy, too, but that reminded her of Alice, so she decided not to.

Her father ordered out for a pizza and asked Ellie to stay for supper, and she said yes, just like she used to, but her father didn't ask Ruthie if she wanted Ellie to sleep over. He knew she wanted to get up first thing tomorrow morning and go to the airport. They were going to have a special breakfast and watch the planes take off and land until it was time to go to her mother's gate.

After Ellie's mother picked her up, Ruthie lay in bed and waited for her father's footsteps on the stairs and his knock on the door. "Enter!" she called, and he sat on the end of her bed.

"Tell me about your day," he said.

"There's nothing to tell," Ruthie replied, and she yawned. "I don't even know where to start." But if she did tell him about her day, she might start at the end instead of the beginning. That afternoon, when Ruthie got off the bus and opened the mailbox, she found an envelope with her name written on it in shiny purple marker. She tore it open and looked inside. There was no letter. Just a heart-shaped amulet, which fell into the palm of her hand.

"Do you want to hear a story?"

"Okay," she said, and she snuggled closer. She was terribly tired, as if she hadn't slept in years.

"There was a girl," he said. "And she lived deep in the forest with a fox who was a shoemaker and a bear who knit striped sweaters . . ."

Ruthie closed her eyes and listened to her father's voice. "Hob-nailed boots . . . golden threads . . . honey cakes." But she was so tired that his words floated in the air over her bed like a baby's mobile or stars, or maybe they were more like Fairy Dust, far away and impossible to reach.